I0682033

Slight Details
& Random Events

Eric Arvin

Published by
Dreamspinner Press
4760 Preston Road
Suite 244-149
Frisco, TX 75034
http://www.dreamspinnerpress.com/

If you purchased this book without a cover, you should be aware that this book is stolen property. It was reported as 'unsold and destroyed' to the publisher, and neither the author nor the publisher has received payment for this 'stripped book.'

This is a work of fiction. Names, characters, places and incidents either are the product of the authors' imagination or are used fictitiously, and any resemblance to actual persons, living or dead, business establishments, events or locales is entirely coincidental.

Slight Details & Random Events
Copyright 2007 by Eric Arvin

Cover Art & Illustrations by HvH
Cover Design by Mara McKennen

All rights reserved. No part of this book may be reproduced or transmitted in any form or by any means, electronic or mechanical, including photocopying, recording, or by any information storage and retrieval system without the written permission of the Publisher, except where permitted by law. To request permission and all other inquiries, contact Dreamspinner Press at:
4760 Preston Road
Suite 244-149
Frisco, TX 75034
http://www.dreamspinnerpress.com/

ISBN: 978-0-9801018-0-5

Printed in the United States of America
First Edition
November, 2007

eBook edition available
eBook ISBN: 978-0-9801018-1-2

For my sisters, Stephanie, Angela, and Amy.

Table of Contents

Acknowledgments

I would like to take this opportunity to thank a few people who have had an influence on the telling of these tales. First and foremost, to my friend HvH (hvhexpo.blogspot.com) not only for his brilliant work on the cover of this volume and the new illustrations herein, but for "Honeysuckle Sycamore" which first appeared as a blog series collaboration between the two of us. I'd also like to thank Josh Aterovis (www.joshaterovis.com) for his kind words in the introduction. Thank you Carey Parrish (www.webdigestweekly.com) for giving a few of my stories their first temporary home. Thank you Dr. Kathy Barbour at Hanover College for inspiring me and easing the poetry and at least one short story contained in this anthology out of my head. Thank you N.C. Strickland for your editing prowess. And finally, thank you to all my loyal readers. You make me constantly want to push myself.

Yours,
Eric Arvin

Introduction

Albert Einstein is said to have once stated, "My religion consists of a humble admiration of the illimitable superior spirit who reveals himself in the slight details we are able to perceive with our frail and feeble mind." In Eric Arvin's *Slight Details & Random Events*, he does indeed reveal his limitless spirit, his strength of character and will. This collection of intensely personal short stories and modern fairy tales will not only entertain and enchant, they will also bring you a little closer to their author.

The heart of the book is a series of connected shorts about Cat and Gael, starting with "The Painting" and culminating with "A Jog in the Rain." In these stories, a young couple struggles to find their place in the world and each other's lives. One of the characters survives a brain injury and its aftermath, much like the one Arvin also survived. Another health scare — this time cancer — shows up in "Raspberry Boy." Both times, the characters fight the despair and fear that comes with such a debilitating experience — and each conquer it in their own way.

For fans of Arvin's first novel, *The Rest Is Illusion*, Verona College, the fictional school that plays such an integral role in the book, makes several appearances. More importantly, the supernatural and spiritual tones of that first novel shine in stories like "Tater 'n Purgatory," in which a young man mourns the loss of his lover. "Camera Phone" also plumbs the supernatural depths, but with a bit more horror. Melancholy stories like "Dismagic Planet" and "The Ice Tree" limn familial dysfunction and death to great effect.

There's something for fans of Arvin's lighter fare like *Subsurdity* as well, including "Absurdity on Jasper Lane." The story is every bit as charming as the book that grew out of it, and it offers a rare and fascinating glimpse into the seed that becomes a novel. The same giddy humor, along with a healthy dose of eroticism, finds its way into a literary triptych starring Gordy, a sweet but dimwitted gym bunny completely unaware of the effect he has on everyone around him.

"Books by Covers" is fascinating and entrancing, quite possibly the best short story I've ever read. The story is centered on a lone jogger making his way through a college campus. It's told through his thoughts, but also internal commentary of those who see him and their reactions to him. "Books" is a brilliant character study.

And finally, there's "Honeysuckle Sycamore," a fairy tale so enchanting and wonderful, you'll wish it wouldn't end. It tells of Passions, supernatural beings born of human emotion, who live and die in a river valley. The story is practically begging to be made into a graphic novel, the imagery is so vivid and rich.

These stories are interspersed with poems and three more short stories. Each reveals a bit more about their author. Who is Eric Arvin? If you don't know already, you will by the time you finish this book.

Josh Aterovis
Author of the Killian Kendall Mystery Series
October 2007

admit it freely

admit it freely: god is a jigsaw puzzle
with missing pieces all over the damn floor
getting caught in the cracks and sliding through the vent
collect them all and you've seen too much and
you'll have to die

god is the big "what"
a neon white glow surrounding the letters
-capitalize now- G-O-D
the great abstraction in glorious abundance:
a freshly painted canvas on the rainy streets of paris
a lion with the laugh of a hyena

still, I want to know

this is my test, like Jacob wrestling with his angel
my birth to the spirit and faith in the world
wanting to believe in the connection
-as a natural being
part of the sphere-
around we go, thrown against other souls
animals and animals
the mingled destinies of crocodiles and men

so I am him and he is me and the world is big
resolution: a jog in the rain

Prometheus

ONE spring morning while walking in the woods that surrounded his home, Jeremiah Bluker came across a man tied to a very large tree. The man was naked and blindfolded with a strip of gold cloth. He sat calmly at the base of the tree. His hands were tied above his head with silver chain link. His large legs were sprawled in front of him, and his goodly-proportioned manhood rested on the ground for all the forest to wonder at. His beautiful, muscular form was undeniable to Jeremiah, who blushed upon looking on him. Jeremiah was a simple farmer, and naked men tied to trees was not something he had ever heard of before. Being that the man was blindfolded, he took the opportunity to let his eyes wander over this marvel of creation. The huge phallus must surely be useless, for no woman could fit it inside her, and no mouth was wide enough for it either. Such abnormalities and the prospects they presented titillated the senses.

"Are you he?" the naked man spoke. He was still quite calm, though helpless and at the mercy of his surroundings.

"Am I who?" Jeremiah asked, approaching the stranger cautiously.

"It *is* you. I know you by your voice."

Jeremiah was certain he had never met the man. He would have remembered such unnatural beauty. Yet his sleep of late had been disturbed. Perhaps he had met this man in the village but by some temporary amnesia was unable to place him.

"I do not know who you think I am," Jeremiah said, "but you seem to be in need of help. I shall undo your bonds. Who tied you thus?"

"You may do as you wish," the beautiful man spoke gently. "But you will be unable to loosen the chain and free me."

"It's simple enough. The chain looks to be only wrapped around and tied to that tree limb." He examined the chain more thoroughly, taking his eyes for a moment off the phallus on its bed of leaves. "Yes. Most easily undone."

"That might be. But you will not be able to accomplish this task. You will be distracted. You always are."

Jeremiah stopped and stared at the man. What a strange thing to say, he thought. Could this man be insane? Was he tied here in the woods, left here, because of some mental defect?

"How did you come to be here? Who did this to you?" Jeremiah asked again. He felt the chains, the smooth and ice of them. He tried pulling and felt some give. But his eyes were beginning to lose focus on what he was doing. They began to wander again, to drift downward in the area of the stranger's crotch. The beautiful man's manhood began to grow like a snake twisting through the undergrowth of the forest. It rose, climbing to an awesome size such as Jeremiah could never have fathomed. And it was stunning. Perfect. A flawless work of art carved from flesh. Veins ran through its neck like azure jewelry. Beneath the great sluice lay a sack of the fullest, most delectable balls. Cannons had not shot balls as large.

Jeremiah tried to restrain his glance, to focus again on the chain, but his fingers no longer cared for that task. They wanted another to keep them busy.

"You are unable, you see?" the man said.

Jeremiah dropped to his knees onto the fallen leaves and grass. "Why am I unable? What is it that draws me to you?" He heard his voice as if in a dream. It echoed and was muffled by a haze of lust.

"Explanations are beyond us. I am your task now."

Jeremiah hardly looked at it as a task. He relished what the man had invited him to do. Something that was forbidden in the village. But here in the woods he was able to indulge. A fever permeated his entire form. He felt his hands hotter for the touch of the man, as if they would scorch the very flesh of the stranger's manhood that was now being touched, stroked, kissed, and licked. As if his fingers might boil the fine, large eggs that he now fondled and brought as best he could into his mouth. The impossibility of it, trying to take the phallus into him in any way he could. He was becoming obsessed with the struggle. The more he was thwarted, the harder he tried. The friction of Jeremiah's attempts at possessing made the thing larger, more gorgeous. Jeremiah was dazzled as the bulbous head of the shaft turned a deep, shining purple and then exploded with a shower of white that seemed not to want to ever stop. Even after that the shaft stood erect, dribbling, and non-defeated. Jeremiah went down again and again. And every time the stranger's phallus would burst into the world its new seed. Jeremiah was insatiable and continued with his play well into the night. He would have taken the man inside him by more pleasurable means if he thought he could survive it.

At last, the jeweled neck became placid, and Jeremiah found his desire too was fading, and he only wanted to sleep. Feeling incapable of finding his way back home in the dark, he curled up beside the chained man, resting his head on the stranger's broad chest.

"What are you doing here?" he asked, sleepily. "Why could I not release you?"

"Explanations are beyond us. We are what we are. We must be satisfied with that."

"You are like Prometheus, I think. Unable to be freed. Drained of your seed every night for some sin against the gods."

"Possibly. But I am blindfolded. If I have sinned, I do not see it." He paused. "And you? Do you see yours?"

"I can remember no sin," Jeremiah said with a yawn. "I'll free you in the morning."

"No, my friend," said the man. "You will forget I am here until you go for your morning stroll. I am chained by some other man's wish, but I remember things. You are free to do what you will, but ignorant. What is your sin?"

Tater 'n Purgatory

PURGATORY was a dog, a real mean dog. He was a dog without a home, without an anchor, but full of purpose. He was dark, gothic symbolism incarnate. At night, he wandered through the woods like a well-fed lupine spirit, having more in kind with those undomesticated hounds and ancestors than ever he did with the pets and guard dogs of suburbia. Purgatory snarled his way through life.

Tate watched Purgatory every evening from under a tin slab that acted as a porch roof on his one-room shack beneath the trees. It is Tate, not the dog, with whom we are most concerned, and whose tale is herein told. Purgatory (named so by Tate because the dog looked like a product of a disagreement between demons and angels) was oblivious to the howls of distress from the creatures he stalked. He tore through elder skunk and newborn wildcat with the same vicious abandon. Tate had even once seen the hound take part in the birth of a batch of felines by gobbling each kitten up as it arrived, fresh from its mother's womb, before consuming the mother as well. This incident might have disturbed the young man if he weren't already numbed by pain.

Tate occasionally wondered in his anguish-free moments if Purgatory had been birthed at all. It was simply more plausible that he had been regurgitated from some rotting earth-hole composed of putrid clay and nether flatulence.

Eric Arvin

Purgatory had been visiting Tate since the young man had moved into the shack, rent-free, a year prior to this story's beginning. Not a word or whelp was ever noised between them. Tate had first believed the animal belonged to his landlord, for whom he did daily chores in exchange for housing. But the landlord, who lived in a big ol' house on the stereotypical hill above the shack, only shot at the dog whenever it went too near his place. Purgatory had never bothered Tate, though. As far as Tate knew, the dog hadn't even ventured within ten feet of the shack. He only stared at it as if waiting for something. Every day, as dusk settled on the wood, Tate sat on a blue milk crate outside his shack while Purgatory would lie miserably on a mound yards away. They eyed one another unflinchingly in uneasy recognition. They saw in one another signs of the crosswalks they had both traversed in Hell.

Purgatory, though a bit of a runt, had never had a problem feeding himself by pillaging the burrows of the forest. Of late, however, Tate noted the dog seemed better fed than ever. In fact, he was twice as wide as he was long. The night was looming closer as man and dog continued their mutual observation of one another. The fading light peeked through the trees, and mosquitoes and bugs emerged from their pits and mudholes to feed their hunger. The owls hooted and small nocturnal creatures made quick dashes from bush to bush. Purgatory was beginning to stir again, shooting a glance here and there, raising an ear whenever he heard a possible pre-meal snack. His stomach made a jarring rumble.

"That dog," Tate said with a smug grin. "He's hungry all the damn time."

"He's a dog," said a comforting voice at Tate's side. "Dogs eat whenever they can. They don't need to be hungry, Tater. Just like you."

"You're always sneaking up on me," Tate said, as he peeped sidelong at his boyfriend. As of late, Tate couldn't even

8

hear Scotty coming. He used to be so aware that he could have heard a pin drop in a thunderstorm. Now it was as if Scotty's feet had grown a thick coat of moss on their soles, as if he just sprang from the earth like God made Adam.

"I don't sneak anymore, Tater," Scotty replied. "No time for that."

"Why you always cavortin' around nekkid as a jaybird?" Tate wondered with affection. "Ain't it bad enough you won't let me touch you no more? Now you gotta make me want."

"Oh, Tater. I don't have time for that neither. It's different now. You know that. I just don't need to wear clothes anymore is all."

Tate lost what good nature he had. His face crumbled into a frown. "I know," he replied. "I know it's different. Wish it weren't, though. Wish there was some way to make it the same again."

He felt Scotty's eyes on him, studying him, wanting him as well. But the line was too thin now; the strained air could not support true interaction any longer. Yearning looks had to suffice for erotic touch. Yet the looks Tate and Scotty fed one another were enough to sizzle passing night flies into nothingness. The humid country night surrounding them was as nothing to Tate's breathing as he looked at Scotty. Tate would swear that he could see his breath; that the summer air felt as frosty as winter compared to what he felt for Scotty.

"The lights are still on at the old place on the hill," Scotty noted, nodding in the direction of the landlord's large home.

"Yeah," Tate observed. "They've been on for days now. He's gone off. I ain't goin' in the house, not anymore."

"You could go take care of the lights. It is your job to take care of things when he isn't able. You've always kept your word before. Ain't no different now. You should go see to them."

"Why?" Tate asked, somewhat annoyed. He leaned away, setting his fist on his muscular thigh. "Why would I do that? It's his own damn fault he left the lights on."

Scotty smiled and let a moment drift by. "Maybe you're right," he said placatingly. "You stubborn son-of-a-bitch." He seemed to relax suddenly, his shoulders dropping as if he were resting on a downy mattress.

"You're leaving now, ain't you?" Tate said, grief slipping through his words. "You're leaving me again."

"I'll be back later," Scotty said with a look of compassion. "I'd kiss you goodbye, but...well..." He lifted his arms in a shrug, and then gradually disappeared into the forest air like a puzzle disassembling itself piece-by-piece.

"You never stick around for nothin'!" Tate shouted to the empty night. Then, more to himself, "All I get is the thought of what was. What it felt like to be inside you." A tear dropped to his hand, and he shook it away carelessly.

Purgatory, who was by this time rife with hunger, rose from his prone position and walked away from the shack, having witnessed Tate argue with the dark. The dog strode, night on legs, through the forest and up the hill. He had no intention of stopping to chase down a squirrel or fox, though he heard many a fretful scamper. No, there was no need to hunt this night. There was plenty of food to be had ahead.

The door was open to the large old house, and the dog entered. The massive man who lay dead on the floor was enough meat to feed him for at least another week. And Purgatory had been feeding on him for only a couple of days, since the day he had been compelled by the odor into forcing his way through the back door. He lapped at the trail of dried blood still surrounding the corpse.

TATE sat alone with the dark in familiar silence. His ears shut out the whisper of the woods; his eyes closed on his burdens. A drunken slumber settled on him, though he hadn't touched beer in over a year.

"Subtract the few worthwhile days from the years, and you'd only live a month," he mumbled to himself. He rose with a groan. It was almost as if he had grown tiny roots all over his body. He felt as if they grasped the milk crate, unwilling to be undone so easily. He was too young, he knew, to have such difficulty rising. He hadn't yet turned 25, but the world had spun around too many times already.

As he walked inside the shack, it suddenly seemed a much brighter place than his single kerosene lantern was capable of showing. It was damn near electrical, but there weren't any electrical outlets in the retired woodshed. He wondered in his vertiginous, lopsided thoughts if he had stumbled somehow up the hill and into the landlord's home.

As he wobbled into the brightness, his eyes adjusting slowly, he saw three figures facing him from the other side of a long table. The table was wider than the shack itself, and Tate realized the walls, indeed the entire shack, had disappeared into the bright yellow light that now surrounded him as far as he could see. Papers were spread out in front of the center figure seated at the table, almost as if Tate were about to be tested or interviewed.

"Sit down, please," said the figure. He recognized the voice immediately.

"*Grandma?*" he stated in shock. His disorientation let his mind more easily accept the ridiculous. "What the... You're as dead as a doornail. I was at your funeral. They damn near had to pry Aunt Janie off your dead body." He slowly took a seat across from them on an old milking stool, nearly toppling back on its wobbly wooden legs.

"Baby, this ain't the time. We got stuff to talk over." She gave him a wink. "We'll talk later," she whispered comfortingly in the manner that grandmas often use.

He quickly shot stunned glances to the figures at either side of her. Sitting to one flank was Scotty, still naked, still beautiful, with a smile as wide as the Atlantic. On Grandma's other side sat a grim, faceless form shrouded in shadows which wheezed and grumbled incoherent curses amidst sickening dribbling noises.

"What's going on?" Tate asked. "I'm drunk, right? But I ain't had nothin' to drink. Mushrooms, did I pick some bad mushrooms? What the fuck!"

"Tater, shut up," Scotty said, his smile still hanging on like the Cheshire Cat. "Now, this is important. They're here for you and me. There are others, too, but you can't see them. It's like a...like a peer review. The thing is, I knew you were coming, so I put in a request that we be matched together. That's what this is for."

"What? That we be together? How? What are you talkin' about, fool?" He scratched his head, completely lost.

"It's simple, baby," Grandma said. "We just need to go through a few forms, ask a few questions..."

"Then we can be together again," Scotty exclaimed.

"Scotty, you're nekkid in front of my grandma! Put some damn clothes on, you nasty booger."

"You're not focusing on what's important here, Tater," Scotty said, exasperated. His smile melted into an expression of annoyance with which Tate was all too familiar. It was the look he received whenever he was being particularly pig-headed or belligerent.

"Now, let's get started," Grandma said, rummaging through the papers in front of her. "It says here you were a couple for around six years. Is that so, sugar?"

"Yeah," Tate said. "Since senior year in high school." He looked to Scotty, still uncertain as to what was happening.

"Messed around for the first time the night of the prom," Scotty giggled.

"In my date's green pick-up," Tate joined in.

"Cause you never got your damn license." Scotty continued to guffaw. Grandma waited patiently until they had both stopped laughing. The shadowy figure wheezed louder as if wanting to tell them to keep quiet so they could get things done.

"And was there any cheating during this time? Any discrepancies?" Grandma at last said, peering over her glasses knowingly.

Tate stumbled. The merriment left him at once. "Um...Once," he said. Scotty grinned and shook his head. "All right! Twice. But it was only because Scotty was stationed so far away. A man needs release."

"You coulda jerked it," Scotty offered. "That's what I did, jackass!"

Grandma clicked her tongue.

"What? What's that mean?" Tate implored. "Why you cluckin' now like a hen?"

"It just means you're a man," Grandma said. "And men are men, no matter who they're pluggin'."

"*Grandma!*"

"Moving on," she said. "How many times have you been in love?"

Tate glanced to Scotty. "Just this once," he said.

"Oh," Grandma moaned appreciatively, putting a hand on her chest where her heart used to be before noting something on the papers in front of her as she nodded.

"Scored some points there," Scotty said.

"Do you want to spend the rest of eternity, every incarnation, every energy level, and every dimension with this man? With this purty young thing sitting beside me?" she inquired.

"Yes!" Tate shouted. "Yes! Without a doubt." Scotty grinned widely again.

"Very well," she said. "Those are all the questions I have. Anyone else have anything they want to ask?" She looked around her as if there were others beyond the yellow light.

"I do," came the gravelly drawl of the dark figure next to Grandma. It leaned forward into the light, and Tate gasped, rising and knocking the milk stool over. His landlord - or what was left of him - peered back at him. His face was bloated and looked half-eaten, his musculature pulsed, stripped of its flesh. He dripped bile and blood everywhere. Grandma leaned away from him in open disgust.

"Jesus!" Tate cried.

"*Why did you kill me?*" the monster grimaced.

Tate stared in horror, raising his arm as if to shield himself from the claws of a demon.

"Gimme a break!" Scotty immediately bellowed at the question. "You know exactly why he killed you."

"Hush now," Grandma said. "Let Tate tell it."

"Well," Tate said, collecting himself and the milking stool. He was quiet as the monster attempted to stare him down - or tried. One of his eyes plopped onto the table with an embarrassing thud, which inadvertently lessened the tension a bit. "Scotty's right, Grandma. That bastard knows why I done it." He put all his attention on the miserable mess of a man now. "I done it cause you done it to me first." He was past the blood and guts, focusing instead on his anger.

"I never laid a finger on you," the man hissed.

"You might as well have done," Tate countered.

"*How?*" he shouted. "I demand to know how? We've never met before this year. Before I offered your sorry ass a place to stay, I never laid eyes on you."

"But I knew you. I knew you way before you knew me. I knew you from what you did to Scotty. When you outed him, when he was discharged because of what you said, he was destroyed. That's all he ever wanted to do. That was his purpose, and you took it from him."

"How is that like murdering a man?" Grandma asked. "Just askin' for the others," she said, referring to those behind the light.

"Because he was never the same," Tate replied, staring at Scotty. "Because, soon after, I couldn't even get him to eat; because his family wouldn't so much as speak with him; and because he hanged himself. His self-worth was so wrapped up in the notion his family had built around military service that even I couldn't compete with it. No matter how much I loved him, I had to watch him die slowly each day." He turned his wrath toward the monster again. "Your death was too easy. Too painless and quick compared to what he endured! And I...I'm still dying..."

"Those were the rules!" the monster shouted. "Those were the rules! I followed them. You had no right to do what you did! That was my life." His voice echoed through corridors and halls unseen.

"No more than you, sir! You destroyed two lives. I think you got off easy, you lousy shit."

"Hon," Grandma said before turning her attention to the monster. "I think your question has been answered." As she said this, the mass of blood and gore collapsed with a croaking moan and flowed out through a hole in the floor like water down a drain.

Grandma gave Tate a wink. "Your mama says hi," she said. Then she disappeared into the dark as the yellow light dimmed, and the shack's sparse lighting returned. Scotty also faded back into the dark, embraced by it.

Tate's sense of the world returned. He no longer felt inebriated or lightheaded. He felt abandoned once more and put his head in his hands, sobbing on the stool, his knees raised so high he was nearly sitting in a fetal position. "Scotty," he murmured. "Scotty. Why do you keep leaving me?"

Suddenly, he felt a touch on his head, a hand running through his hair, and he looked up slowly. The electricity of the touch told him who it was before he even saw Scotty beaming down at him. Immediately, Tate jumped to his feet and embraced his companion. He held him as tightly as he could, wanting to feel every muscle either of them possessed contort, flex, and respond to the corresponding muscle in the other.

"Scotty," Tate cried. "I didn't think I'd be able to touch you again. Not until I was dead and gone." He cradled the back of Scotty's head with his hands.

"But, Tater," Scotty said, pulling away a little. "You *are* dead."

Tate stared into his eyes, confused. Scotty nodded in the direction of the open doorway, beyond which hunkered the night. Through the door, Tate could see someone seated on *his* milk crate. Reluctantly loosening his grip on Scotty, he approached the door cautiously. He became aware, in a moment of slow realization, that he was in fact still seated on the crate. There was no one else there; he had never risen at all. He had been dead for quite some time, and his vacant eyes stared out into the woods after the phantom of a wounded, old dog. They had lost all reflection; he was the soul peering back into the empty body which had housed it. Yet he had no desire to stay and guard the lifeless corpse against those who would befoul or besmirch it.

Tate held Scotty around the waist tightly as they headed slowly away into a promising new night. "I'm not gonna lie and say I'll miss who I was right there at the end."

"Good," Scotty said. "That's Hell, the not letting go."

"I think I let go the day you died, Scotty," Tate confessed. "I was just waiting around for my walking papers."

"What do you say we take a stroll under the stars? That's a romantic thing to do, right? They say so in the movies."

"What about my body? Will somebody find me...er, it?"

"In time," Scotty answered. "Do you care?"

Tate thought for a moment, none too heavily. "No, I really don't," he answered. "Let's go get romantic."

Eric Arvin

Camera Phone

HE didn't know why they had even bothered to come. They were in the nosebleeds, so far away from the stage, so high up, that they couldn't even see the gyrations of the hot male dance troupe. But the tickets were free – a promotional tool from a local radio station – so Marc and his boyfriend had said, Why not?

Gay men and straight women hooted and hollered around him in the balcony seats as if they could see clearly what was going on down below. Thankfully, Marc had brought his camera phone with him, and he could zoom in on the action. Security was lax, and he could easily get away with it. Cell phones were so tiny these days, almost unnoticeable.

On stage danced an especially well-hung firefighter. A costume cliché, yes, but who cares? This wasn't Broadway, after all. This was burlesque. Marc took out the camera from his jacket pocket, looked around for security, then quickly snapped a photo. It was an exhilarating thing to possibly get caught, but nobody saw him. The audience was too busy ogling the sweaty, humpy dancer.

Marc looked at the photo, prepared to see something gorgeous and muscular. Masturbation material much better than some porn rag because this guy was real. Not touched up. What he saw puzzled him, however. The stripper was there, quite evident in all his shiny, muscled, well-endowed glory, but there was another figure as well. Someone shadowy and strange.

18

Someone who had not been on the stage just a moment before. A tall, thin man with pale skin stared at the stripper, unmoved. The stripper seemed aware of some strangeness near him. He looked anxious, uneasy, avoiding the thin man's gaze.

Was there no security around at all to keep creeps like that away from the dance troupe?

Marc looked to the stage again. There was only one man there. Just the beefy firefighter whose movements now seemed slower, as if frightened and ready to bolt. The audience was becoming aware of his lack of attention to his performance. A few boos came from the crowd.

Where was the thin man?

Marc raised the camera phone again and clicked, completely forgetting to check his surroundings for security. The picture he got this time startled him even more than the first. The thin man appeared once more, but now he was no longer watching the stripper. Instead, his eyes were focused on the audience. Staring up, in fact, to the nosebleeds. At Marc.

Marc's heart began to beat faster. He looked around him nervously. His boyfriend, noticing his anxiety, asked him what was wrong. He said, Nothing. Nothing. Just dazed by it all, I guess.

His boyfriend nodded in naughty approval and returned his attention to the stage. "Make sure you get some killer pics," he said.

Marc swallowed and clicked again. There was a blur in the new photo. It passed directly in front of the stripper. The thin man was caught mid-leap from the stage by Marc's camera phone. The hairs on the back of Marc's neck stood on end. His breath quickened. What was happening? Who...what was that? Didn't anybody else see it? Surely he couldn't be the only one in the audience with a camera phone.

Click.

The stripper was alone now. The thin man was gone. The stripper seemed to recover. He put more oomph into his struts and moves, and the audience responded with frenzied cheers.

Click.

Still nothing. But the stripper was much more comfortable.

Marc began taking pictures of the entire arena. To his right, to his left. The thin phantom man had disappeared altogether. After a while, Marc relaxed somewhat. He began to enjoy what he could see of the show again. He and his boyfriend laughed and whistled at the parade of muscle men who disrobed in front of them, and he nearly forgot about the strange, pale, thin man.

On stage now was a fine specimen of masculinity. A very large man whose best asset, it was clear, was his rather amply-sized backside. He jiggled and bounced his rear at the audience, and it went wild. Marc could not resist getting a picture of that. He might even blow it up wall-size!

Click.

When he looked at the photo, he went pale. He felt his blood as ice, his hair as pin pricks. He almost forgot to breathe at all. In front of him, blocking the view of the stripper, was the thin man. He stared directly into the camera, his eyes as dark as coal, his face emotionless and gaunt, his lips thin and tight. Marc stood with a start. Those around him did as well, but because they were caught up in a frenzy of lust, not a surging terror. Marc looked at his boyfriend. He wasn't paying attention. He was too busy fantasizing about the muscle god on stage.

Just breathe, Marc. Take it easy.

Click.

The thin man's sickly hand was reaching for the camera phone. Marc jerked, as if the phantom in front of him could actually take the phone from him. His teeth were chattering now.

He couldn't stay here. He told his boyfriend he'd wait for him in the lobby.

Are you okay? This guy's hot.

I don't f-feel well.

He stumbled over men and women who were unaware, who could not see. As he went, he snapped pictures. Nothing. He kept using the phone, all around. Nothing. A calm started to settle in again, though he continued to walk with a brisk pace. Maybe he had left the thin man behind. Maybe whatever it was – a ghost, a demon – maybe it only haunted the arena.

Marc went to the restroom. He needed to get the image out of his mind. There were a few men there, but they hurried about their business so that they might get back to the show. Marc splashed some water on his face and stared into the mirror. His entire body visibly shook. He was barely able to lean on the sink – his arms quaked so that his elbows felt as if they might give out.

Calm down. Calm down. Whatever it was, it's gone. Maybe you're hallucinating. Maybe you took something you shouldn't have.

He needed to know. It frightened him, but he needed to know. Just to make sure, he took another photo.

Click.

He screamed when he saw the picture. In the mirror, behind him, a thin, pale face rested on his shoulder, fitting perfectly into the curve of his neck.

Dismagic Planet

TODAY will be like yesterday, I suppose. Same shit, different date. Hoping for anything new, anything different, is useless. I can't even remember my dreams. Haven't for two years. I know I have them, dreams. I heard once everyone has dreams; that they would go crazy without them. I don't think I'm crazy. I'm just a teenager; that's too young to be crazy.

Dew, my brother, died last month. A whole month since what I call the Incident, and it still feels it's just happening. The moment, the paralyzing realization of what I'd done, is always just coming to me. Like shards of ice surging beneath my skin.

I've also heard that dreams are the soul's adventures when it leaves the body at rest. If I ever had a soul, if I still have one, it doesn't wander at night anymore. It remains with me or else has died and withered inside me.

Every morning for these last couple of weeks I wake up empty and dreamless and smelling cinnamon. Mom bakes a lot lately. Too much. There are only the two of us after all. She doesn't say anything. At least not to me. Cinnamon bread therapy or a distraction from her only living son. Take your pick.

She's always in the kitchen. The goddamn heart of the home, right? And I'm always upstairs in my room, sick. A floor divides us. We find other dividers if we need to. The rooms in this old house aren't big enough for the two of us and what we carry.

Her resentment crowds my remorse. In my room, I stare at the ceiling for purpose – or the Hand of God, whichever comes first. Purpose would mean contentment, happiness. But since the Incident neither of us are almost "perfectly happy" anymore.

Rising now from my bed. Rising to the smell, the awful sweetness of the cinnamon bread. I turn my head in that slo-mo style. Sometimes I think my neck will snap if I turn too quickly. (It's not death that frightens me, it's the getting there.) Staring dully out the window of my upstairs room, I see it snowed again last night. It's snowing still. Some poet somewhere is probably in love with the world this morning. It's a pure, reaching, expansive blanket. Clean, untouched. The purity forces me to look away.

Then I think, how will I find the dog under all that snow? Dew's dog. His best bud all his young life. I've been looking for it for a few weeks now. It disappeared soon after the Incident. It had to be dead. It wouldn't have run off. Dead, just like Dew – dead as Dew. Ten, he was only ten years old, and I...

Dew died, dog gone. Makes me laugh. It's wrong, but it makes me laugh which will make me cough, which will make her bake even more. She won't come to check on me. I haven't heard a knock on my bedroom door in over a month.

I must find the dog today. I have to. To lessen the pain. To numb it. Maybe if I find that dog, maybe then it will make this place, this house, this dismagic planet, seem okay – a little.

I'm going downstairs now. Descending. My descension. She's manic at the sound of my steps, wrestling with metal pots and pans. Clanging, banging, bong bong bong. She's in her world, in the kitchen. Busy, busy cinnamon clears her head. I know to avoid her eyes. She does the same. We're ghosts that can't see one another. She's perfected the art of avoidance. She's done it longer than me, since Dad left. I know she wishes she could find the soul she had when she was sixteen – when nothing was terrible or wrong, and bad things never happened to good people.

23

But then, maybe we're not good people. Maybe we've both slipped.

What did she think when she heard that shot? Did she pray for the first time in years? Or did she think it was probably already too late to pray? God's gone to bed. He's not watching anymore.

I remember standing there. How reality bent and deformed and nothing seemed real. That could not have just happened, I thought as my legs began to tremble. An impossibility to lose anymore of the magic than had already been taken from us.

No use in praying? Probably true, but it wouldn't have hurt, would it?

Walking into the kitchen, trying to force her to acknowledge my existence a little. Avoid, avoid. If we spoke to one another our words would be distant and out of sync with our mouths like some badly dubbed foreign film. Nightmarish. This is where my dreams go, into the kitchen. Maybe my dreams fester here unused and become nightmares that smell of cinnamon.

I am sick. So sick.

In my coat and outside, I am blinded by the snow. I am glad to leave the heaviness, the stifling, of the house. She is glad to see me go. I swear it, as I left I heard a sigh of relief from the kitchen.

The inches of white crunch beneath my feet. I'm leaving canyons behind me. They'll be filled in again soon enough. The snow is falling heavier. Quiet snow. Stand still and hear nothing. Not a car on the highway or in the world. Silence forever. Crisp air, like the crackling of a fire or a shot.

I go marching up the lane, looking for the dog. Trees, weighed with ice and snow, droop and lean over the hidden gravel road. Brush too near to a limb and *snap!* The whole branch falls, splintering down with a pain almost too familiar.

Playing around. We were only playing around like boys do, and there on the table, next to the closet door, was a gun. A nail gun. Mom was using it to permanently close the closet where Dad had stored his things. He didn't take anything with him. I never even saw him leave. I didn't know what it was when I picked it up. Just grabbed for something as we played. Dew had this toy rifle pointed at me. Boys and war toys. I pointed the nail gun at him. And shot it like a stapler. Didn't even know what it was. Straight into the brain.

The dog, where's the dog? She will never forgive me if I don't find that dog. She will never forgive me.

I see something in the woods. Looks too big to be the dog. I walk toward it. The snow is loud against the mute world. Whatever it is, the sound of me approaching will surely disturb it. But I notice blood. There's blood all over. It's been skinned clean and raw. A twisted mouth, sagging eyes. I gasp from familiarity. It's alive. It's looking right at me. Sees everything I don't want to. It's reaching for me.

Sadness. This is what grief would look like.

I run.

Once back at the house, I rest. I can't breathe. What sadness would look like. Sadness in need of mercy. Pleading for forgiveness. A howl soars from the silence. As if the wind has been wounded, winter harmed.

Where's the dog?

THANK god, he left. Thank god he's gone for a bit. I can't be near him, can't look at him. Just smell the cinnamon, the sweetness. The smell covers everything. Feel the dough. Soft and delicate.

Nothing messy. Everything under control. The dough is clean, rolled out flat and flawless. I can make things new every time I bake.

He'll never find that dog. God, I hope he never finds that dog. I'm not sorry I did it. When I killed it I felt nothing. I just could not take the moaning and crying and bellowing. I could not take the reminder or the competition. He was my son. I loved him more than some animal. You don't have to wail and carry on to show pain. To show that you care. To let the world know you are a mother.

Roll the cinnamon bread. I'm a good mother. I'm a good mother.

Decapitated dog, suicidal mother

Suicidal son who killed his brother

Brother in a coffin so near to his father.

autumn jazz and dad

the taste and smell of memory (*breathe deep and speak*) are
the senses of autumn; the taste can be bitter, but the smell
(*breathe it in*) is grilled hot dogs, football leather, pumpkin
and patchwork pies in puddles; autumn is a relief from
constrictions, and everything - even a tree - will exhale

[he said he would live forever; he and god had always known it
  the chainsaw goes back for seconds and thirds, and you
  and your brothers are there; it's the same every autumn
  the bitter taste of sawdust and resentment; *oh my god,*
  he'll live forever, even as his hair turns a strange silver]

autumn falls into a sigh, big and laudable; leaves change to become
paper-money, worthy of exchange; night breezes are drugs - euphoric
and like angel-water (*breathe that in at least*); and slowly,
seeming to be suddenly, it's a melancholy moon and cornstalks turn to
gold when touched by the headlights; looks like jazz - *you* need to hear
some jazz

[when winter drifted in you were so busy pondering on the
  disappearance of paper-money and angel water that you forgot,
  forgot to listen to the beauty of footsteps - his heavy feet on the
  kitchen tile, until he collapsed on the bedroom floor and couldn't
  live forever anymore, proving god and the world wrong]

the headlights strum the cornstalks making imperfect jazz, filling that need
silent jazz: *rustle-rustle-rustle-hushhhh*, you can hear a voice sway
through this harmony; he is whispering (and god is whispering), *nothing*
to forgive - and you...**breeeeeathe**; you in rhythm with the
cornstalks' jazz; autumn smells of pumpkins and tastes of molasses

...and silence is so accurate.

27

Eric Arvin

The Painting

THOUGH it seemed as if the snow would never stop falling, spring at last finally arrived to Verona College. Spring term at Verona was basically a party mixed with a shot of education. For the entire month of May students were only required to take one class, which they attended every day for a couple of hours. Since most of the student population opted for less stressful courses, there was ample time for drinking and enjoying the warmer temps. It was a time during the school year when everyone was for once in a great mood. For how could they not be, surrounded by the beauty of the campus along the river?

Cat and Gael couldn't hang out as much during the new term because of Cat's baseball schedule, but Gael did what he could to make sure there was no lull in their burgeoning friendship. A friendship that began with an innocent look from Gael (innocent enough, anyway) at the college dining hall the first week of classes. On weeknights there was a wiffle-ball tournament sponsored by one of the fraternities on campus, which was basically just another reason to get drunk and play ball at two o'clock in the morning. Cat and Gael would participate in the madness whenever Cat had no baseball games the next day. When he did, Gael never failed to show up for them. He felt no shame in the fact that he was jealously guarding Cat against any unseemly sorority gal. Too, it was a great way for Gael to relax and watch scattered ass from the bleachers. Cat looked amazing in his uniform, sporting what Gael referred to secretly as the best baseball ass in the state.

As the weather warmed and the campus greened, Cat and Gael had also taken to jogging around the small school. The hilly paths and roads provided a great way to stay in shape. Their workouts together at the college gym had paid off, and they were eager to flaunt themselves topless and tan past classrooms and college visitors.

The class Gael had chosen to interrupt his pursuit of pleasure that term was actually a lot of fun for him in and of itself. It was a course in painting, and most of the course work was out of class. Gael found that painting, like writing or exercising, gave him a wonderful natural high. Midway through the term the class was given the assignment to paint something describing their moods at that particular point in their lives. At the moment Gael was content, if a little worried that everything around him was going to suddenly be ripped away. But content doesn't make superlative art. His favorite colors had always been fall colors and, being the melancholy poet that he was, he decided to paint something with them. And he knew exactly what he wanted to paint. After hesitating briefly, Gael nervously asked Cat if he wouldn't mind being the subject. There was no hesitation on Cat's part; he agreed right away and with a smile that kept Gael upbeat and chipper for the rest of the day.

That Saturday afternoon they drank and goofed off in Gael's dorm room as they had done many times since they had first become acquainted. Cat sat shirtless in a pair of black boxer briefs, straddling a chair. Gael directed him, telling him to rest his head on his arms which were folded over the top of the back of the chair. Gael, shirtless as well for no real reason, painted with his back to the window so as to get a good dose of sun on the paint and let him see clearer. The entire painting took the span of three hours with plenty of frivolity and alcohol breaks included. Halfway through the painting Gael was completely drunk and made what he thought to be a daring artistic move. Instead of keeping to the autumnal theme of the rest of the abstract painting, he chose a pretty blue for his subject's head. Trailer-park blue. It was the most artistic thing he had ever done. A shade of happy blue mixed in with oranges and browns and slight yellows all done with very broad brush strokes. At six in the evening Gael put down the paint brush and sighed happily.

Cat rose from his straddled position and walked around, beer in hand, to view the painting. "That's awesome," he said quietly. "You got real talent, boy!"

"Well, I can't take all the credit. You see, I had this most intriguing young model...." Gael said, trying to sound grand and aesthetic. He stood and stepped back, eyes still on the painting.

"It looks sad... I look sad." Cat looked at Gael. "But I'm not sad. I'm having a great time."

"Well, I had to emote...um, an emotion...." Gael smiled. "I was emoting, you see. All art, I think, is a lie."

"I gotta be honest, it's a downer. A buzz-kill."

"Good. That's what I was going for. I guess I just painted a lie, huh? Cause this ain't my mood right now." He laughed.

"It's nice, though. The painting, I mean. I like the blue. Leaves it open to interpretation maybe. Kinda like hope or something."

Gael could hear the relaxation in Cat's voice from alcohol consumption. The ball player stood behind the painter as they both studied the painting. Gael felt warm breath on his neck. Then he felt a finger gently, ever so slightly, glide up his spine and sweetly descend down again. It was a continuous motion. Gael shuddered with pleasure. Ease and relaxation rippled through his body. Not being able to stop himself, Gael turned to face Cat. Cat put his hand on Gael's shoulder, and in a moment of complete surrealness, he kissed him. To Gael, the feeling of Cat's full lips was heaven and satin and silk and every redundant overused phrase he could think of. In fact, there needed to be a new word for what it was like to kiss Cat. Gael's entire body felt like it was about to burst into flames. Not smoke and cinders, but high flames come from a fire goddess; straight from Pele's hands. As Cat held Gael close to his own flesh, Gael could feel the heat and he savored it as if he were freezing for warmth. It felt as if the nerves in every inch of his body had evolved into quills and were trying to break through his skin, but in a ticklish, glorious way. There was no doubt this was lust.

There was a battle going on in Gael's head as they continued to caress and kiss. He was confused about how to feel. On the one hand he had a sweeping, orchestral score sailing through the corridors of his mind; theme music to the realization of a dream. But then there was that dark, locked door behind which were all his fears incorporated in him by the godly zeal of his father. That theme music sounded more like *Jaws*. In the end, though, he opted for the sweeping melody of desire and fulfillment. But, as was always the case, his guilt could not be silenced...and he sneezed. Every time he ever got sexually excited, he would sneeze! It had been happening since he could remember.

"Are you all right?" Cat laughed. They had made their way over to the bed. Gael was humiliated. His own inner turmoil had ruined the moment for him.

"Yeah. Just a little embarrassed. Sorry about that. I didn't spray all over you, did I?"

"Not yet," he grinned widely. "Allergies?" he asked.

"Actually, it's kinda weird," Gael said. "Truth is, whenever I think about sex or get really excited...sexually, I sneeze." Gael stopped. Cat was laughing hysterically. "It's not funny!" Gael protested, trying to suppress his own laughter.

"You're right. You're right. I'm sorry. Man, that religion really fucked you up, huh?"

Gael just smiled and looked to the floor.

"So are you gonna keep sneezing? Should I get a face-guard?" Cat chuckled.

"Very funny. No. It only happens once, then I'm good."

"Well, then, let's get back to it," Cat said as he cupped Gael's face and they kissed. "You know what the Bible says: 'God loves a cheerful sinner,'" he whispered.

"'Giver,'" Gael whispered back.

"What?"

"It's 'God loves a cheerful giver,' not sinner."

"Same difference," he said as he pushed Gael onto his back.

From there they continued to get better acquainted. Gael's hands traveled down the length of Cat's arms and back until his fingers were massaging Cat's perfect ass. Gael felt Cat hard against him, ready to push in. Gael slipped his hands into Cat's boxer briefs, feeling the rounded muscle of his ass. Cat breathed harder and pressed into Gael more deeply and urgently. At that Gael grabbed the briefs slid them down Cat's strong legs. There was a tattoo, a butterfly tattoo, on Cat's right thigh and Gael became enamored of it. He traced it with his fingertips and then ran up the inner thigh until he heard Cat moan quietly. Now Gael was in control. He pushed Cat back onto the bed, and they spent the rest of the night there. For both of them, it was all as fresh and new as the wet painting that faced the window. Gael felt as if he had been a swimmer kept too deep in the pool who could finally come up for air.

Eric Arvin

The Things We Want

THE fraternity house was on the very edge of campus near an overgrown patch of woods that hid the narrow, winding, treacherous drive that was once the main road onto college property. It had since been abandoned because of the dangerous inclination among the young students to speed and the stubborn propensity of the hulking boulders that surrounded it to fall. The house itself was regal, yet it looked almost overcome and defeated by the surrounding trees. It was as if the vines and roots of those withered giants would imminently wrap themselves around the old fraternity and drag it into the dark netherness that secret old, places have always held.

During the school year, the house was a lively place and looked proud and unique among the other, more conventional Greek houses on campus. The trees behind and around it also served a purpose in the eyes and hearts and groins of the brethren. The old arbors and the air that surrounded them were known to emanate a very relaxing odor in the hours between midnight and dawn. Needless to say, the woods allowed ample cover for ne'er-do-wells and the rest of us to play the way we do in the dark. A guy could get away with a lot living so far from the heart of campus. Wants and needs of the most carnal kind could easily be obtained.

School was out for the summer, though, and the house appeared saddened and alone when I first saw it. The vitality given to it by the students who had lived there had been sucked away. The fraternity looked weary of the trees that reached toward it with their crooked, knotted limbs. It was clearly going to be a heavy task for Cat and me to bring life back into the old house as we cared for it for the season. Our pay was free room and all the leftovers in the kitchen. Of course, we had other jobs on the side.

The weather was muggy and oppressive. Sweat dripped from us like molasses as we worked that first day on our living arrangements. We brought all the fans we could find in the house (those left behind by the brothers) and assembled them in the house director's room where we were staying. There was no air conditioning. The brothers' house money was spent instead on parties and pledge events.

That night, after all had been moved in or about, Cat and I laid siege to the room in hedonistic abandon. Everything that we considered to be responsible – or could be construed as such – had been done earlier. I had worked at the fitness center 'til noon, done my workout, and then gone on my cherished dusk-light jog with Cat. He, for his part, had gone into town, rented some movies, and purchased anything we might need, which included a bottle of gin.

We began drinking early. It was still very hot in the room, so we set the fans to circulate in our direction. We had the volume on the TV turned up almost as far as it would go to cover the roar of the fans, but we still perspired. Colleges in river valleys are extremely humid.

Cat sat on a recliner with one leg stretched over one of the arms of the chair. He had stripped down to his tight briefs. (A cute boy in his underwear. If there's anything better, I don't know of it.) He held a tall paper cup of 7-Up and gin, as did I.

"This is sweet," Cat said in a lazy tone. "Ain't this sweet? Just us. None of those wise-acres to jump around and holler."

"Yep," I agreed. "It's the simple stuff. I mean, who needs it."

"Needs what?" he took a large gulp from his drink.

"All that...crap," I said gesturing to the TV as it flashed random images of things neither of us might ever be able to afford. "Nobody needs all that." I could feel the slightest effect of alcohol on my senses already.

"Who can afford it?" he retorted. "I need gin, a good baseball game, and I need a fan when it's hot..."

"Lots of 'em," I interrupted.

"But you're right. Who needs the rest?" He said it lightly – almost too lightly to be heard over the army of fans.

"The rest of the guys in the house seem to like their little gadgets," I said. I had seen their mp3 players and iPods scattered about, left behind as if they had cost nothing at all.

"Yeah. But they probably didn't have to buy those. Most of the guys are better off than I am."

"I wouldn't say they're better off," I said, sensing the slightest hint of envy in his voice.

Cat looked at me and smiled. "No. You're right again. But they have more money, and that makes things easier, I suppose." He strummed a hand down his sweaty abdomen, wiping away some bug or sweat bead. "My daddy never had nothin', and he turned out fine. Worked his ass off to get me here."

I wanted to say "me too," but the truth was quite different. My father had died before college had ever entered my mind. And besides, his religious inclinations would have been against socializing with the world outside my childhood, the world which I had escaped. Maybe I would share that tale with him some day...but not this day.

We left the lights off as it grew darker, leaving just the TV to illuminate our surroundings. The night came on like a thick woolen blanket. The heat never let up. But we had our fans, and I enjoyed hanging out in my underwear with Cat. It was as close to being intimate with him as I had ever been. We drank gin, watched movies, and sang along to music from the assorted CDs the house director had left behind for the summer. When Cat slipped in Ricky Martin, we both got up and did our best at dancing, though neither of us had anything resembling rhythm. It was simply a chance to let loose in the summer night. I was in my blue boxers, Cat in his tighty-whiteys, and both of us were shaking our butts. Cat definitely had considerably more booty to shake – he was a ball player, after all. It was a moment of heightened excitement for me when my hand "accidentally" brushed his ass.

We then collapsed into our chairs and welcomed the wind-makers on high. Dancing was fun, but it was definitely hard work in this heat.

After a while, things started to get a little hazy for both of us. Gin, the Green Fairy, took complete control of our faculties. I could see Cat almost drifting off. He looked sweet, almost innocent.

"Man, I'm gonna crash," he slurred.

Like a child being told to go to bed, Cat rose from his chair a little hesitantly. The alcohol had impaired him tremendously. Realizing, I suppose, that his bed, which was a high bunk, was not a remote possibility that night, he slowly felt his way to the carpet at my feet. The fans surrounded him like watchmen or tiny windmills. There, he curled up in the fetal position. The itchiness of the carpet didn't seem to bother him at all.

I did not wait for an invitation. He looked too precious. I rose from my own seat as smoothly as I could, turned off the TV, and descended to the carpet as well. I didn't hesitate as I pushed my body against Cat's clammy back, spooning him as if we were

Eric Arvin

two boys on a camping trip in the back yard huddling together to keep warm. The sweat between us mingled. I felt my own heated breath on his soft, tanned, strong shoulders. It would have been a perfect moment if not for the damned gin muddling things up. It was as romantic as I could have imagined. My arms wrapped around him slowly, my fingers strumming his abs. It was a moment as precise and sharp as the fan blades.

"What do you want from this?" he asked, startling me as he broke the silence. I thought he had already fallen asleep. "From this life, I mean. What do you want to get from it?"

I was a little relieved that he had restated the question. At first I had assumed he meant to know what I wanted from him at the moment, with my arms around him and the hardness he now surely felt pressing against his backside. I was readying to loosen my grip and shrivel away like a salted slug before he asked the question again more clearly.

"I don't know. I want a lot of things, I guess. Too many things. Mostly things that don't matter." I stopped. Material things, contraptions and gadgets, popped into my head like those I had seen earlier on TV. But was that the answer? The real answer? "When it comes down to it, I guess I want to be content like everyone. Why? What do you want?"

"Two things. I only want two things from life," he said. "I want to travel, and I don't want to die alone."

I could tell he was drifting off to sleep from the tone in his whispering voice. But his quiet proclamation had awakened me a little. I raised my head so I could more clearly see the side of his face shadowed by the night. He was peaceful and beautiful. What he said had made me see him differently, though. I had been given an inside look at the miracle. He had shared with me an insight into his fears. I was moved almost to the point of tears.

"You're not going to die alone, Cat," I assured him. "That will never happen. You're going to live forever, and I'll..." but I

38

stopped there and swallowed my thoughts. I'd tell him some other night...but not tonight.

"As far as traveling, there's a course in Italy next spring term," I whispered. "Maybe we should look into it."

"Today was a good first day, huh?" he whispered. "A great first day of summer."

I could have replied but he wouldn't have heard. He was asleep. So instead I stole a kiss from behind his ear.

I rested my head back down on the carpet, and I breathed once again, happily, on Cat's smooth shoulder. There were so many things I wanted to say to him, and for the first time it looked as if he might understand. I wanted to explode my secrets all over him. But I kept those words for later. At the moment, for as long as I could keep my drunken eyes open, I would enjoy the feel of him in my arms. With my heart racing, I hugged him like a pillow.

Everything I had to tell him, all my wishes, had to wait until morning...or some other day. Maybe later in the summer. Yes. That would be best.

Eric Arvin

Italian for Beginners

FLORENCE. *Firenze*. An intoxicating blend of creepy romantic antiquity and intruding modern style.

We were finally among its citizens and tourists. The months of begging Cat had won me this. Weeks and weeks of wearing him down until, finally, he had said with faux exasperation, "Fine, Gael! I'll take the damn class!" And he did. He dismissed his intended plans for spring term of our senior year in college, and we went on the first real trip we would ever take together.

For me "getting there" was not so much fun as it was a slow torture. My excitement was stupidly high, and it dawned on me the experience might be a letdown after the buildup in my mind. I shrugged it off, though, and continued to ready myself for the day we were to leave.

Besides, I convinced myself, *everything in life is a bit of a letdown*. Nothing is ever as blissful as when it's first imagined. Nothing at all survives the collapse of its initial illusion.

THE skies had clouded, and it was raining upon our arrival in that much adored Tuscan city. The plane flight had been long with interspersed conversations and snoozing. I sat next to Cat and woke up once on his shoulder. For once, he didn't seem to mind the open display of affection.

At the airport we were loaded onto a bus, then swept hurriedly through the antique streets. They were dimmed, and the colors dulled by the overcast sky.

Arriving at the B&B, we were shown our small and cozy rooms. The room Cat and I were given rested at the very end of a stream of hallways branching out one from the other like a maze. Certainly, it was unlike the design of any place I had ever stayed. (It wasn't until later I learned the building was, at one time in its long history, a monastery.)

Class was held from morning until noon every day, which meant we had the rest of the day to see Florence. We were given assignments, but nothing so hard as to keep us away from the culture around us. Culture was, after all, the very reason we were there.

There was a lot of adventuring, mostly done in large, cautious groups at first. Everything we were supposed to see – everything it was a sin not to see – we saw. It took some time. Long lines and heat were a deterrent to some. Cat and I were usually on our own, taking more adventurous routes down other alleys and purchasing souvenirs of questionable quality from sketchy, eye-patched, yet strangely attractive venders. When we would find a bar or pub (which was often) we would go in, have a drink.

The sexuality of the city, the sheer steamed heat, was overwhelming. *It was marvelous!*

Cat and I wore our most form-fitting clothes. We soon discovered it was uncouth to wear tank tops in Florence. That was an automatic indicator of ripe "Americaness." So we adopted the darker, more sleek style of the Florentines. Aside from being very hot, very uncomfortable, we looked great. The sleeves of our tight black shirts would stop at the biceps of the arms, making them seem even rounder and harder than they were. Cat's arms bulged from years of playing baseball.

Eric Arvin

BEING left alone by most of the others who had taken the course was a plus for Cat and I. It allowed us more freedom to explore the city to our own liking and not be fettered by the conformity of others' wishes. We didn't ignore the others, nor they us. We were all friendly and pleasant to one another, but the fact was, neither Cat nor myself had ever befriended or hung out with any of those in the group. Not one among them was in either of our circles back on campus.

On my birthday, which makes its appearance in the spring, untethered by our classmates and their often embarrassing rhotacism, Cat came up with the idea to search for a gay bar in Florence. I was shocked! *Cat was wanting to visit a gay bar?*

"You do realize there are homosexuals there?" I teased. "Ho-mo-sex-u-als."

He laughed at me, then slugged me on the arm. *It hurt.*

"It could be fun," he said. "I'd never go to one back home, but nobody'll ever know here. It's your birthday! You should be...gay."

So that was it.

Again, we dressed the part of two single men about town and walked the busy evening streets of *Firenze* with butterflies in our stomachs. It was early yet. The night had only just begun. Children were out with other children, and families were strolling the piazzas and buying gelatos. Cat had found directions to a gay bar nearby via the internet with the one computer the B&B had installed just for guests. We scoured the entire piazza looking for this hidden den, but were having some difficulty locating it. The address given led us to a dark alley with a large steel trash bin. We were completely at a loss. There *was* the thump and beat of disco music nearby, though, so we knew we were in the right area.

After a short while we gave up and decided to ask for help. Directly across the way was a gelato parlor. So I mustered all the American courage I could gather, and we approached it nervously.

The owner said something to us from behind the counter. He didn't smile. He was a harsh-looking man with jet-black hair, a square, unshaven jaw that could crush bone, and coarse skin.

I was petrified.

I presented the white tablet paper on which Cat had written the name and directions of our destination and pointed at the unfamiliar words. At once the gelato man seemed to lighten up. His initial impression had been but a mask, and now his true face, the smiling fatherly visage of gentleness, was shown. My fear melted like a raspberry gelato on a hot, Italian cobblestone street.

He said, "You?"

Cat and I looked at each other then back to him and nodded. His smile was so *good*. It was just... good. A person could drag out any thesaurus, any word-finder in any language, and there would never be another word which would describe his smile better. *Good*, because that's how it made me feel. It reminded me of my father.

Still grinning, he lifted his heavy arm and pointed us back to the way we had just come. We were confused, but he insisted. So we walked slowly back to our original position, cautiously looking back at him with every couple of steps. By the time we reached the dark alley again we could not make out the shop owner's face, only that he was still watching us.

Then, at last, we saw the entrance to our destination thanks to another patron's departure from the joint. The heavy black door clanged shut behind him. Cat and I were in complete wide-eyed amazement at what we saw. The great steel dumpster, the trash bin we had previously laid eyes upon and thought little of, was not a dumpster at all. No, in fact, it was the very cleverly hidden front door to our night's main attraction. It *was* the gay bar! The music, which was now clearly something more techno and mechanical than disco, pulsated louder. The streets of old Florence for a moment turned as rude and raucous as any American nightclub.

Smiling in something akin to disbelief, we approached the ominous looking door and looked for a handle. At not finding one, Cat shrugged and knocked. In seconds a slit in the door appeared and two menacing eyes glared at us. A voice yelled something at us from inside in a heavy *un*Italian accent that possessed none of the lyricism of the locals. There was a fiendish, red glow around the eyes of our watcher.

"Wonderful," I said to Cat out of the corner of my mouth. "Welcome to the Gates of Hell."

The eyes from inside yelled something once more, at which point we began to slowly back away, then hurriedly turned and walked away to *anywhere* else.

"What the fuck was that?" Cat burst out laughing as we made our way out to the center of the piazza.

"I have no idea, but if that's a gay bar I'm done with 'em," I said, still wide-eyed and grinning.

"It was like an evil secret society. Or like they were afraid the cops were going to bust them." We kept up a brisk pace. "Are they called 'cops' here?"

"The first thing that popped through my head was the Emerald City. When that door slit opened, you know. Like an evil Munchkin."

We continued to walk about the city that night, eventually going to a more comfortable nightclub and drinking to my birthday. Afterwards, we stumbled back to our beds, just barely making the curfew set by the B&B. We cuddled and drifted to a semi-restful sleep but for the thought of two leering and evil eyes that kept making us chuckle and laugh.

The evil Munchkin mayor. A gnome of the gay underworld. (Shudder.) What would our parents have thought? Could they have ever imagined it?

NOT all of our classes took place at our kindly B&B. There were trips to familiarize us with the other places referred to in our assigned readings of Dante and Petrarch. Day trips were spent in

Siena; in the gorgeous walled city of Lucca; Pisa; and the seaside resort town of Viareggio.

Our final week, though, was spent in the Eternal City of Rome. This was the grand aspect of the entire course trip. To see Rome was a dream. Cat could barely contain his excitement. I was sure I could see a constant erection through his blue jeans. The Coliseum was his only point of reference as far as Rome was concerned, but then he would have gone for that alone. I knew of other things, but only in small fragments. Short phrases and names of places I wasn't even sure were correct.

We arrived in Rome and were taken by another bus to another B&B. Almost diagonal to the building was a small alley where, at night, little shops were set up so as to lead one to the open festival that was just beyond in the piazza.

The Piazza Navona was a celebration of Rome every night. As I stepped those few yards from my occupancy to the alley and then into the piazza, it was as if gates were opened. One felt like a hero coming from the shadowed back street into the openness of the piazza with its shops and restaurants, Bernini's Fountain of the Four Rivers, and his rival Borromini's church of Saint Agnese.

I pointed out to Cat, knowing his interest in such things, that the entire piazza had at one time been the stadium of Domitian. I had just learned that little fact myself, but didn't tell him this. If he thought of me as Clio, the muse of history, I had no problem with wearing that fabulous cloak.

The first full day in Rome we had no class. Everyone was free to amble and discover at will. We all, of course, wanted to see the same thing: the ruins.

What I saw was every film, every book I had ever read about Rome. It was all the clichés and images that come to mind when a person thinks of Rome. There in the morning sun was the Forum Romanum and the Arch of Septimius Severus. We walked among the broken stones and cracked monuments that were the glory of the ancient days. I marveled at them, but, at the same time, I couldn't take it all in. I was trying to hold the experience and harness it, but the moment was too big for me.

The same sense of bewilderment and humility, of respect and incomprehension, remained with me at the Coliseum. Cat, of course, was in awe. We were in the midst of ghosts and echoes. Thousands of them.

Toward midday, Cat and I split from the group. While the others walked off in search of food, the two of us followed our cheap, already wrinkled and torn map of Rome and headed for the chariot track. Cat walked excitedly, quickly. I was soon breathing hard trying to keep up with him. It was getting very hot, and I had the uncomfortable feeling of sweat dripping down my sides.

"Ben-Hur!" Cat said, looking out on what was now an unremarkable park for lovers and dog walkers. Only the faint oval of the track remained. The Circus Maximus, built by King Tarquinius Priscus to mark the spot of the rape of the Sabine women.

Cat gleamed at me. He flung down the backpack he was shouldering and retrieved his camera.

"Take a picture," he said. Onto the track he ran, arms raised overhead like a lunatic. All the while he yelled, "I'm Ben-Hur!"

At first, I couldn't get the shot, I was laughing so hard. The people in the park didn't seem to mind him. Silly Americans probably did this sort of thing all the time.

"*I'm Ben-Hur! I'm Ben-Hur!*" he continued to scream, as he ran the entire length of the track. I sat down on a knoll and waited for him.

Satisfied with his adventure, he returned to me, breathless and grinning. In all my life, the cutest sight I ever saw was Cat making believe he was a Roman on the Circus Maximus.

IN Rome, it was very hard for me to wake in the morning. This was because it was very difficult for me to get off to sleep at night. When were in Florence, Cat and I had the luxury of our own room. Without intruders we cuddled and fell asleep together, fumbling through sticky indulgences in the night. I was so used to feeling his soft, muscled, warm body next to me all a jumble with mine, that the bed in Rome seemed hard as stone.

Too, we shared our room with two others from the group. A couple of fraternity brothers who were incessantly talkative. I was going through Cat withdrawal, and all I could hear as I tossed and turned was chatter. Did he miss me as well?

When the two frat brothers rose from bed early Sunday morning, waking me up in the process, I wanted nothing but absolute vengeance. They were rattling on about going to mass at the Vatican and seeing the Pope.

"There's a rumor he'll be there!"

Just a rumor, and they were all jumpy, jittery, and excited. He was to canonize someone.

"A whole slew of people!"

Well, wonderful. Let him get to it and let me go back to sleep.

They couldn't believe I didn't want to go. I just rolled over, clutching the pillow to my weary head.

Cat was less peaceful. He picked up the guide book that lay beside his bed and threw it at one of them, then turned back on his side in a grumpy huff.

WE did, in fact, at last reach the Vatican during the week. In the Basilica, we walked among the gold and statuary. We marveled at the columns. How enormous they were. Everything was so ornate. The Christian god, it seemed, was a flashy fellow.

"I read somewhere that if you walk through the doors of St. Peter's all of your sins are forgiven," I said as we strolled like ants among the giant columns.

We stood looking at Michelangelo's *Pieta.*

Cat sighed. "I'm gay," he said quietly.

"What?" I almost laughed. It was the first time I had ever heard him refer to himself as being gay, admitting to it. I thought he would forever be the straight ball player who sleeps with guys.

"I'm gay," he said again, loud enough for those around us to hear.

I didn't bother to look for shocked expressions.

Cat looked at me and smiled. "I can admit it, and it's okay. I'm gay."

"You're telling me this in the Vatican?"

"Yeah. I know. I see the irony. Kinda cool, huh?"

"Coming out in St. Peter's Basilica? I'd call it something close to lack of respect if I believed in this god."

"But you *don't* believe in this god...and why are you whispering?" His hands were in his pockets, and he turned to look at me with a swinging motion like that of a fidgety kid.

I looked at him and a wave of adoration rolled over me. "You're right...baby."

"Tee hee," a faux laugh, "You just called me 'baby'."

"I'm very proud of you. You're one in a million, Cat," I said.

"Thanks." He whispered for the sake of intimacy, leaning in to kiss me softly on the cheek.

"SYDNEY? *Australia?*"

The words came from his mouth like dead weight and hit the Roman air with a thud as we walked near the Spanish Steps. I had been trying to avoid that particular conversation until we had returned to the States, but Cat had asked me again what I was doing next year. Which school had I chosen for graduate studies?

"Why are you going so far?" His tone was more accusatory than inquisitive.

"I've always wanted to go." My words took on a slight tremble. "I think it will be a good experience. Classes don't start until after the new year. I'll still be around until at least February."

"You weren't going to tell me about this until *when?*" He looked like he wanted to hit me.

"I wasn't sure...I wasn't sure how you would take it. I wanted to tell you." I tried to speak calmly and keep him from boiling over. I had never seen Cat truly angry.

"So you just let me yak on about going to school back home while you were planning to get away? To get away from me? I thought we'd be near each other." We had stopped walking and were near the base of the Steps. "Am I a delusional fool here?"

"Listen, we weren't even that serious when I made these plans. All year long it's always been about keeping things secret. About not letting your buddies know about us. How could anything get serious? You're always so fucking worried about keeping things secret. I feel like nothing more than an undercover fuckbuddy sometimes!"

"Oh, *I'm sorry*. I forgot you're the goddamned patron saint of gay college students. So you're more comfortable with it than me. Two points!"

He leered at me, and I was speechless. Now I wanted to hit *him*. I turned and began to walk quickly away. He followed.

"Aren't you going to say something? You're so good at standing up for yourself; your ideals. You're going to run from me *now?*"

I turned and faced him. "Shut the fuck up!" was all I could manage. My mind had gone red and then blank. I was furious. *Cat was yelling at me!* How had it gotten to this? One moment we were at the Spanish Steps, and the next, a conversation about grad school had escalated into an argument. The faces of the passing people vanished into a white raging nothingness.

Suddenly, my eyes were drawn to a surgical scar on Cat's shoulder. It's all I could see.

"You're right," Cat said, his voice taking on a mocking note of calm. "It wasn't serious. Maybe I'll hook up with one of the girls from class."

"They see through you! Everyone knows you're gay! Everyone knows you take it up the ass like a little bitch faggot!"

49

Had I said that? I couldn't believe I said that!

Cat set his jaw. "Watch yourself, Gael," he warned me.

"I think I would like to be by myself."

He looked at me a moment, then smirked, raised both hands and backed away, palms out. I wanted to stop him, but my pride was in the way. So I turned around and began walking, the shops speeding past me as I peered blindly ahead. My mind was lost in a bad dream.

He had raised his voice...*to me.* Why couldn't he see? Why wouldn't he want me to see Australia? He was jealous, that's what it was, he was jealous. I was going to go off to see more of the world, and he was stuck. He would always be stuck!

I don't know how long I walked in this oblivious manner. There was no purpose or destination in mind.

As I continued walking, I began to intuit a strange feeling. I was being watched. I heard the stop-and-go of a vespa, and I was in no mood for this new nuisance.

Across the road, a man seated on a vespa was staring at me. His helmet and sunglasses prevented me from getting anything descriptive from his appearance. He was dressed in black, though, and it made me a little uneasy.

I ducked into a nearby shop – bags and such – hoping he would cease annoying me. As I pretended to peruse the various satchels and backpacks, in he came. I watched him out of the corner of my eyes. He walked with long, heavy, careful strides – as if he were looking for prey. How long he had been watching me?

"Hello," he said in a voice that did not seem to match his frame. It was too light and a bit too high. "American?" he asked.

"Yes," I said with some hesitation.

"I am art student at University. You please model for me."

"Model? Oh no...no, thank you," I said.

"Please. I am very good." He loomed large over me, like one of the many ancient columns that dotted the cityscape. His presence was a perfect capper to an already odd and frustrating day. He pleaded with me more. The sane thing to do was walk away, but I was not feeling particularly sane. The argument with Cat had made everything feel different.

In a moment of splendid surrealness, I stood among expensive leather bags and agreed to model for the stranger. Everything blurred all the more. I felt like a spectator to my own actions. It wasn't me getting on that vespa with my arms holding tight to a tall Italian's chest. No, it couldn't possibly be me whizzing through the streets of Rome dangerously fast.

What was I doing?

None of that mattered at the time, though. My body had been overtaken by some other spirit. All I was thinking of was Cat and our disagreement, and, strangely, that scar on Cat's shoulder.

I was thinking of all this as I got off the bike; as I got in a lift and rose a few floors above the city to a studio apartment. My kidnapper had removed his sunglasses and helmet to reveal a shaved head and brown eyes.

The strange bald Italian talked continuously, telling me about what it was he did. The apartment was very much like one would expect an artist's place to look. There were many fine art books and prints, along with knick-knacks and obscurities artistic people seem to be drawn to.

Adriano (that was his name) led me to the bed. I was asked to remove my clothes as he got a sketch pad and pencil. There was no protest from me. The moment was too out of normal boundaries for me to say much of anything. So I lay nude on the bed as the artist sketched away. There was no shame or embarrassment. I felt, in fact, numb.

After a bit, Adriano put down his pad and came over to the bed. Slowly, he knelt down between my legs and swallowed what had become hard. I wasn't turned on, but sexual organs seem to have a mind of their own. He sucked and pulled with such a ferocity that I slowly became aware of some discomfort through my numbness. There was no enjoyment or climax. I wasn't interested in Adriano, and he was getting frustrated that I hadn't come yet. But that was never going to happen. He wasn't Cat.

With that thought, I began to wake up from my surreal state of being.

Across the room I heard a sound; a machine. Like a camera or camcorder readjusting itself, refocusing. It hit me: *I was being taped!*

I jumped up, pulling my dick away from Adriano's hands and mouth.

"What was that? Are you taping this?"

He looked dumbfounded. In truth, I wasn't looking for a reply. I grabbed my clothes and ran for the lift.

It was getting late afternoon as I began my journey back to the B&B. I had no idea where I was. Yet, I would find my way. I was certain.

My mind was completely awake now. The discontinuity that had clouded my thoughts had gone, leaked out of my ears and evaporated into the air. I was finally able to sort things.

Yes, I should have told Cat.

Yes, I knew we were becoming serious.

What of Adriano? Should I tell Cat?

I spent hours walking and thinking until at last I saw familiar architecture. A gibbous moon shone overhead as I finally entered in sight of the B&B. It would have been a wonderful night to play with Cat in the Piazza Navona. But that was lost now.

I walked in the front doors and up the stairs, then past my sleeping classmates' rooms. I opened the door to my own room cautiously. Cat was awake and sitting up in bed. The frat brothers had gone to sleep. I stared at Cat from the doorway with one hand frozen on the doorknob. Tears began to well up in my eyes.

Oh, don't be that *guy,* I thought, chiding myself. *Don't be that sentimental guy.*

Cat nodded in recognition, then slid down and turned over on his side.

THE next day we were all packing to return home. There wasn't much talking between Cat and I. Only half-smiles and nods. Things were in need of repair, but it was too soon to start. Everything would be talked out later.

"What's wrong? You two lovers have a fight?" joked the brothers.

Cat picked up the guide book and once again hurled it at the guy, nailing him on the forehead.

"Fuck!" the injured young collegiate screamed.

Cat and I grinned at each other and continued packing.

Tension be damned, we sat beside one another from bus to plane. There was no question whether we would.

Airplanes had always given me headaches. On the flight home, though, I really didn't notice. The noise level of the plane and its passengers were of no concern. What truly concerned me was the quiet and lovely guy next to me. I would glance over at him nervously, and Cat would do his best to ignore me. Occasionally a grin would escape from his stoic demeanor. Our arms touched gently on the armrest, his fine arm hairs brushing against mine any time the plane jolted or shook.

"Sorry...baby," I said at last. There was more to be sorry for than he knew.

No response. My words were met with unmoved profile.

The fasten seatbelts sign popped on as the cabin shook. Turbulence ahead.

Eric Arvin

Electronic Love, Australia

Hey Baby!

From our conversation on the phone after the flight, I could tell you were still edgy about my being here. All I can say is that it's only a year program. I'll be back soon, and with a master's degree. (I think you're just pissed that your degree is going to take twice as long. Just kidding.) Please don't get all sentimental on me like you did when I left *ever again*. Evan helped me through the first hours of missing you... well, Evan and Starbucks. I'm glad she came with me to Australia. Oh, and about Evan, she thinks you hate her. What's that about? Please write her and tell her it's not true. Anyway, better go. Evan and I need to find a hostel while we search for apartments near campus. I'll e-mail every day. There's an Internet café on every corner here. It's amazing! You and I both know neither of us can afford phone calls right now. Like I said before I left, though, I promise to call once a week AT LEAST.

Love you and miss you!!

Gael

God I miss you! And it's only been two days since I saw you at the airport! I'm a pussy.... Anyway, no, I won't write Evan. The fact is I do hate her, the bitch! Just joking (or am I?). I'll write her as soon as I'm done here. Classes are going okay where I'm at. Cold as fuck, though. I can't believe it's summer over there. So weird! I mean, they have Christmas on the beach. Sounds sweet.

I'm glad I got to spend this Christmas with you. Mom really liked you. Thanks again for finding that Willa Cather first edition. She loves it. Valentine's Day was my favorite, though. You and me in my apartment on the sofa all night. I love that it snowed. GOD, I MISS YOU!

Well, babe, I gotta be getting to class. You're a day ahead down there, right? So if I want to catch you on Friday night that means I need to call early Friday morning? You're always ahead of me. Overachiever!

Love you Baby!!

Cat

Hiya Dollface!

Been here a week now. It's so strange. This city is massive! Sydney feels larger than any place I've ever been, and yet I know Rome has to be larger. Evan and I stick pretty close for fear of getting lost. As I told you in our lil' weekly phone splurge, the hostel is nice. They say we can stay on as long as we need. Usually there's like some time limit. A certain length of days and then you're out, but this is apparently not a busy time for them. Summer is winding down now, after all. The hostel has an Internet café located in it, so that makes things easier. Last night Evan and I went to the roof where they have set up a nice picnicking area. We got a couple of alcoholic beverages (against the rules, by the way) and watched the planes landing and taking off from the nearby airport. It's all very pretty, though a bit loud. Tomorrow we're going to sign up for classes. (I told you the hostel was right down the road from the University of Sydney, right? In fact our road leads right to the University park.) Afterwards, we're going to check out some more apartments. I hate having to go through a realtor to find an apartment. I don't trust them.

Oh! One more thing. I forgot to tell you about this flight attendant on the long flight over. He was checking me out. I mean, really checking me out. I was wearing that black sweater you got me for Christmas. Well, the guy looked more like a rugby player than a flight attendant. He was hot! Anyway, he kept chatting it up with me. He even brought Evan and I a couple of those gift thingys from first class. When we were about ready to land, all buckled up, he says to me "You're very cute"! I didn't know what to say! I retorted with a clumsy "Thanks." I just thought I'd pass that on to you. It was amusing.

Who loves you, Baby!

Gael, that's who!

Whoa!!

Are you already forgetting about me?! Keep your pretty gay hands off those rugby-playing flight attendants! You have no idea how jealous I just got reading that. I'll admit it. I got jealous. I've decided that I'm going to come visit you. I have gotta see this place for myself. Don't know when. I haven't fixed a date in my head, but it'll be as soon as I possibly can. I'll start saving now.

Things here are pretty much the same. It's still very cold, but the weather guy says everything is going to warm up next week. We might even hit a balmy 50 degrees. School is everything I thought it would be. Very, very dull. I'm beginning to think I went into the wrong area of study. Maybe I should just join the army or (hee hee) the navy like my dad. Mom says 'hi'. Oh, and do you remember Blake Parcel? Big guy, chubby, really nice, but smelled like rotten tomatoes? Well, he sent me the strangest letter today. I'm not sure, but I think he's telling me he's gay. Did you ever get a vibe from him while he was my roomie in college? I bet he was trying to look at me naked! Dang homosexual!

Yours truly (who will be calling your ass this weekend to interrogate you on said flight attendant),

Cat

Great news darling!

Sorry I haven't written for a couple of days, but we found an apartment! Actually, we found lots of them, but this is the only one the realtor will let us have, and we still had to haggle over the rent. AAARGH! Anyway, it's a two-bedroom second-floor apartment in a really nice area. It has a balcony, crown moulding, and a security buzzer-upper thing, like on *Seinfeld*. (Unfortunately, it also comes with what seems to be a very large family of cockroaches. We're told, though, that Sydney has a cockroach infestation problem. It would be the same anywhere. Yuck.) We are actually located in a suburb of Sydney called Coogee. It was once a resort community. We can see the beach from our balcony. It's a good spot to sit and check out the surfer boys and sun-tanned studs. There is plenty of eye candy here (though none compare to you, darling). There's a nice little café by the beach that Evan thinks should become our morning tradition, and a fitness center right outside our door. It's all kind of perfect, actually. I can't wait for you to see it all!

Classes are going okay. It's so much easier than I thought it would be. I guess going to school at Verona really paid off. How are things going with your classes? Has it gotten a little more interesting? Spring's just around the corner (for you anyway), just keep that in mind.

We finally got a small CD player, so I was able to listen to the CD you made me. I love it!

I miss you! I miss that purty mouth o' yours. And I miss that ass. I jack off to it every night (wink).

Lata figure-skata!

G

Sooo happy to hear you like the CD. But then, why wouldn't you? I have great taste. "Pancho and Lefty" was my favorite song on the CD. Gotta love Townes van Zandt! (Your gal Emmylou does a great cover of that tune, by the way.)

I'm so jealous that you are out on that beach all the time. When I come for a visit I think I'll be spending most of my time on the sand...well, there and the bedroom (wink wink). But please, I don't want to hear anymore about the surfers! Enjoy them in silence. As for my own ass that you alluded to, I'm keeping it fit for you. I joined a baseball team. It's an amateur league here in the city. Nothing big, but it'll keep me in shape.

Grad school is fucking dull. I hate it! Nothing new to report other than the fact that it's becoming a little harder. My grades are slipping of late. I'm just not interested in anything they are teaching me. I'm thinking of taking some time off after this term.

Blake and I have been spending some time together. He's really nervous about the whole gay thing. He's even more closeted to his friends and family than me. He does look better, though. He doesn't smell anymore, either. He makes me a bit nervous sometimes. I think he might be flirting with me. I don't know how to let him down easy. I've told him about you and me, but he doesn't seem to care. Don't worry, though, I'll keep him at arm's length.

And get this: Mom is trying to set me up with some girl in her church. The pastor's daughter!

Anyhoo, gotta git. Talk soon, baby. Love you!

The C-man

Okay. I don't really know how to ask you this, but my mom is really pressuring me to date the pastor's daughter. I think she's getting suspicious. She's always asking me why I don't have a girlfriend. What do you say to me fake dating her? Not for real. Just like a show for my mom. Just for a bit.

Cat

I get that you're upset. I tried to call back after you called me, but I know you're pissed off and probably chose not to answer. I'll try again tonight. We can talk this out. It's just that Mom is asking all these questions. You had every right, though, to call and scream at me. I'll talk to you soon, I hope.

Love

Cat

Baby! Please answer the phone! Or at least e-mail me again!

Love

Cat

Thank you, thank you, thank you! That phone call meant a lot. Finally speaking to me again, huh? It was so great hearing your voice. I realize that breaking that news to you through e-mail was probably not the best way to go. No matter now. I'm going to tell Emily that I'm gay. I did tell you that's the pastor's daughter's name, right? Emily. I'm doing this for you, but I have to get Mom off my back somehow. Any suggestions?

Cat

Kitten,

I'm glad to hear that Emily took so well to your coming out. I can't believe, though, that she wasn't attracted to you. Impossible! Yes, I suppose it would be okay for you to be her show pony... or she yours. Whichever the occasion calls for. So I guess Rosa is pretty happy then, huh? Her son is "dating" the pastor's daughter. How long are you going to keep the charade up?

Anyway, been hanging out with some guys from England. They're all obscenely wealthy and bumming around Australia for a year. They're a lot of fun. The two I've taken a liking to are Ewan and Liam. (How original, right?) All they do is go to the beach and then travel on the weekends. They stay in hostels, but I don't understand why. They can afford much better accommodations. They play rugby near the beach a lot of the time. Evan and I will go down and watch. They asked if I wanted to play, but there's no freaking way! Those guys kill each other! American football is for out-and-out wimps now that I've seen this game.

Forgive my jealousy and childish behavior over Emily.

Love you!

Gael

Blake Parcel killed himself. Heard the news yesterday morning. That's why I didn't call. I went and visited with his parents after I heard. Some of the other brothers from the fraternity came to see them as well. I don't really know how to feel. I knew him, but not extremely well. I lived with him, but we didn't share too much. In the last couple of weeks we hung out, and everything seemed great. He was even talking about putting his pic on one of those Internet matchmaker sights. Everyone is puzzled as to why he did it, but I think I know. He was going to tell his family he was gay. Maybe they didn't react the way he had dreamed they would. Baby, this scares me. What would happen if I told Mom? I'm going to call you tonight.

C

How was the funeral? Stupid question, I know. Are you feeling any less uneasy? I wish I could be there for you. I'll call later.

Love you,

Gael

Thanks for the pix you attached to your last e-mail! Damn you look good. Down Under agrees with you. I'm in a better mood now. Blake's death just put me in a deep funk. It's been over a week now, though, and I think I'm getting back to normal. Went down to visit Verona, our alma mater, last weekend. Walked to the Point and sat and stared at the river. It did me good. The weather's nicer now. Just sitting there I felt refreshed. You know that Joni Mitchell song where she sings "I wish I had a river that I could skate away on"? It kept running through my head.

Missing our jogs,

C

Have I got a story for you!

Evan and I went out partying with the Brits last night. Everyone got sloppy drunk, and, after the Redcoats had stumbled off to their hostel, Evan and I too went to bed. Well, in the midst of my drunken slumber I am awakened by a figure in my doorway. (I always leave my bedroom door open.) I was terrified at first, but then realized the thin frame to be Evan. She was taking off her clothes! Not slowly either, but as if they were on fire. She then came over to my bed and mumbled something. I couldn't understand a word. Aside from that her box was directly in front of my face! That's right! Her naked-to-the-world VAGINA was staring right at me! It was terrifying... and completely shaven. I didn't know where else to look. How do you avoid looking at something like that? So then she ran to the door of our apartment and tried to open it, all the while mumbling something that sounded like "I know we know, I know we know." I watched as she ran to her room, then back to the aforementioned door. This back-and-forth went on for about 20 minutes. I was getting very concerned. When I tried to stop her and ask what was wrong she said (finally something coherent) "It's in my blood." What?!

Eric Arvin

What kind of nutcase had I agreed to lease an apartment with? "It's in my blood." Was she on drugs? Sleepwalking? She finally succeeded in getting the apartment door open and going out naked into the hall. She was ready to climb down the stairs and go outside but I dragged her nude ass back up. Well, after about an hour she calmed down and laid on the couch. I stayed watch for a bit longer, just in case. I covered her up with blankets and went to sleep. The thing is, she doesn't remember a thing about it. I'm freaked out. Do you think somebody might have slipped her something? Liam and Ewan were with her most of the night. Either of them maybe?

Anyways, how are you?

Love

G

Hello Lover!

So Evan thinks her lunacy the other night was a combination of mixing her medication for depression and alcohol? Whatever. It's still a little funny, though. Tell her to take it easy.

Emily and I are the perfect fake couple. Everyone is none the wiser. Emily's dad, the pastor, is happy that his daughter is dating such an upstanding, moral boy. Emily needs me for show as much as I need her, it seems. She's had a boyfriend for a while, but has had to keep it secret because her father disapproves. I'm in a big, fat cliché but it's working for me. Mom is ecstatic. She's already making wedding plans! She's come down with something. A cold or flu bug, but not even that can keep her from reveling in the fact that I'm dating the pastor's daughter.

Love

Emily's show pony,

Cat

It makes me a little sad to think that neither your mom nor mine would be as ecstatic about planning a wedding for the two of us. Everyone says they want happiness for their children, but it's selfish, really. How will marrying so-and-so make the family look, or will they have children for the relatives to spoil? I don't like this Emily girl. Not one bit. It should be me and you, not you and her. Why can't people be happy for us?

Classes stink. One in particular, Ancient Roman History, is so full of pompous Eurotrash students that I feel nauseated stepping into the room every day.

Later

G

Cheer up darlin'. Things will get better. You only spend a few hours a day with your classmates, and then you get to spend the rest of the day with people you actually like, right? And about the wedding thing, it's a ridiculous tradition. Weddings always lead to divorce and anger. Ask my mom about that.

My classes are almost ended for the year. I'm still debating on returning next term. We'll see.

I'm definitely coming to visit next month. I put the plane ticket on the old credit card. I'm so excited to see you again! I'm gonna call tonight.

C

Hey baby.

I've been feeling very ill the last few days. I don't really know what's wrong. I don't have a fever but I have the symptoms of the flu. A few of them, anyway. It started after I hit my head the other night. Evan and I had the Redcoats over and Ewan, drunk off his skinny little ass, jumped on me. I lost my balance and my head hit the corner of the wall. There was a bit of blood, but everyone assured me it wasn't serious enough for a doctor or stitches. I guess I should have gone anyway. I have gauze wrapped around my head. I'm sure it'll start a trend.

After it happened, as I sat there cradling the back of my head, Evan and Liam were making out right in front of me. I was a little pissed off! A little concern might have been nice. I actually thought at the time it was a bit more serious than their drunken minds could fathom. I still do. I might go see a doctor.

I'm through with drinking, Baby. Done.

Is Rosa feeling any better?

Love

Gael

Sorry for the frantic phone call. Didn't mean to wake you, but you had me scared. Are you feeling any better? I can't believe you didn't go to the doctor right away! I know I reamed you out about this on the phone, but it was a really stupid thing not to do. Oh, and is it okay for me to hate Evan again?

About the drinking prohibition: I agree. I think it's a good time to stop. Maybe we've been drinking too much as it is. Actually, there's no 'maybe' about it. I'm gonna stop right along with you. Moral support.

In other news, I fake broke up with my fake girlfriend Emily. Mom is devastated, but she'll get over it. I'm tired of having to act all lovey-dovey around people. Emily told her dad about her real boyfriend. That's what broke up our faux relationship. She got angry with her father and just blurted out that she was cheating on me with another guy. I'd say 'bless her heart' if I were religious. She took the fall. She's the bad guy. All I get is sympathy. She doesn't really give a shit, though. She and her man are moving in with each other downtown, and they're happy.

Of course, I have to act upset for a while, but at least it's over now. I can move on to other girls, you know?

Well, take care. Call me tonight. I want to know how you are doing.

C

God, I feel awful. I thought I'd feel better by now. In fact, I feel worse. I'm sick to my stomach. I can't keep any food down. I think that's due in large part to this acute dizziness, vertigo, whatever it is. I lay down, and the room just spins. Sometimes it feels as if my eyes aren't catching up with my head when I turn. Also, I have this loss of strength. My grip and strength in my wrist seem to be lessening. I'm a sight to see, Boyfriend. I hate going out of the apartment because I just get so disoriented. Like I'm lost in the world, like I'm on the wrong planet. Everything has a dream-like quality. It's a nightmare! On the bus ride home from campus today I lost my balance and fell over on some chick. The driver took off before I could find a seat. She gave me the dirtiest look. I'm not myself anymore. I am completely changed.

Mom wants me to return home immediately. I know she's worried sick. I want to see if I can fix this and stay here, though. I really like it here. I have an appointment with a doctor at the Prince of Wales Hospital.

Thanks for the daily calls. They keep me looking forward to things. Mom too. She calls every day as well.

Love, and talk soon.

G

COME HOME!!! You sounded terrible on the phone. I know you love it there but you have got to think of your health. You can come back and get well, then go to school somewhere here in the States. The fact that your leg seems weaker and your ankle keeps giving out worries me. You would feel better back here in the States with people you knew. Those few you've met in Oz can't be of very much comfort. They don't know you like we do. Evan will just have to find another roommate. Vomiting every morning is no way to start your day. Besides I need you here to help me fend off my mother. She wants to set me up with another girl.

Please come home. I'm supposed to come down in a couple of weeks, but I might see if I can get on an earlier flight to drag your ass back!

Love you and want you home!

Cat

I had a CT scan today. I hate those things. I remember my Dad having to deal with them when he got sick. They're so loud and uncomfortable. I have another appointment with the doctor to discuss them. Dr. Phelps is his name. Nice enough, I guess. He smiles a lot. It makes it seem things might not be that bad. I know that's not the case, though. I'm still as ill as ever. Vomitous and gross. I haven't been able to work out, and it's showing. I sleep a lot and try to keep from falling. I'm missing all my classes. I haven't the strength to travel to class. It takes 45 minutes from Coogee to the university. I don't really care about my studies anymore. My profs are e-mailing me their worries. I'm missing too much, they say.

Evan isn't really that helpful. She's pulled away. I don't think she deals well with illness. She had a brother who died while she was in high school. He had some disease and lingered for a few years in a coma before he passed away. I don't really try to ask too much of her. I know how uncomfortable it makes her.

Anyway, I'll call and let you know about the results from the scan. Talk soon. Keep writing me. It's the thing I look forward to most every day.

Love

g

Don't you worry about me not writing. I'll write five times a day if it'll cheer you up. Evan needs to grow up! I know for certain I hate her now. I'll be coming to see you in a couple of weeks. Have you given any more thought to returning home? I think it would be for the best.

As for my educational adventures, I, too, am missing classes. My reasons aren't as acceptable as yours. Simply put, laziness and boredom are keeping me away from my seat in the lecture halls. Also, I'm finding it hard to concentrate on anything. You and your dilemma are always on my mind.

I'll write you later today, and I'll call. How's that? Something to look forward to, huh?

Keep well and keep your spirits up,

c

You get your ass back to class! No excuses for you! I'm kidding, of course. I understand disinterest. From our phone conversation it sounds like you are probably just unsure of direction. Maybe a year or so out of the halls of academia would be just the thing for you. I'm off to see the doctor about scan results. I'm a little scared.

Love

Gael

Cavernous hemangiomas. I looked it up on the Internet. There's some sites you might want to look into. I'll e-mail the addresses to you later. Just because your father died from it that doesn't mean anything, does it? It's not always fatal like that, right? God, I wish I knew something to say. I'm so frightened for you. How did your mom react? I couldn't do anything today. I just sat around my apartment and tried to figure this hemangioma thing out.

I quit school. I can't do it anymore. I got a job as a manager at a GAP. I start this weekend. What are your plans now? I know the doctor said this would work itself out in time, but do you still plan to stay in Australia? I should have asked that on the phone. Write me back ASAP.

Love

Cat

Can you get a refund on your ticket? I'm coming home after all. I've already booked a flight. I'll call you tonight with the details. Mom was so relieved when I told her. She's even flying out to meet me in L.A. Then we'll fly back home from there. Evan is helping me pack. She's started looking for a new roommate. I hate to leave, but I know it's the best thing to do. This morning, before anyone was stirring on the beach, I went and sat on the sand. I enjoy just watching the water lap at the shore. I put some of the sand in a little bottle. One of those tiny ones that hold samples of liquor. I'm taking it home with me. I'll stick it up my ass if I have to. Part of Coogee Beach is coming back to America with me. I'm not going to the beach again before I leave. That was it. Well, I'm tired, and I can only type one-handed now (I have no strength or flexibility in my right hand), so I'll say goodbye.

Later baby.

Gael

I'm so happy you are returning! I know you're feeling like shit right now, but things will get better. It's the way life is, right? One day it's smooth water, and the next you've hit the rapids. I'll take care of you. I'll drive down every day to see you. My mom's sick again too so maybe the two of you can get together and bitch and moan. (Kidding.)

Your mom called me like you asked her to. I'm meeting up with her in Verona, and we'll fly out meet you in L.A. Everything's gonna be okay, Baby. Nothing lasts forever. Good things will always trump the difficulties.

Can't wait to see you!

I love you so much!

Cat

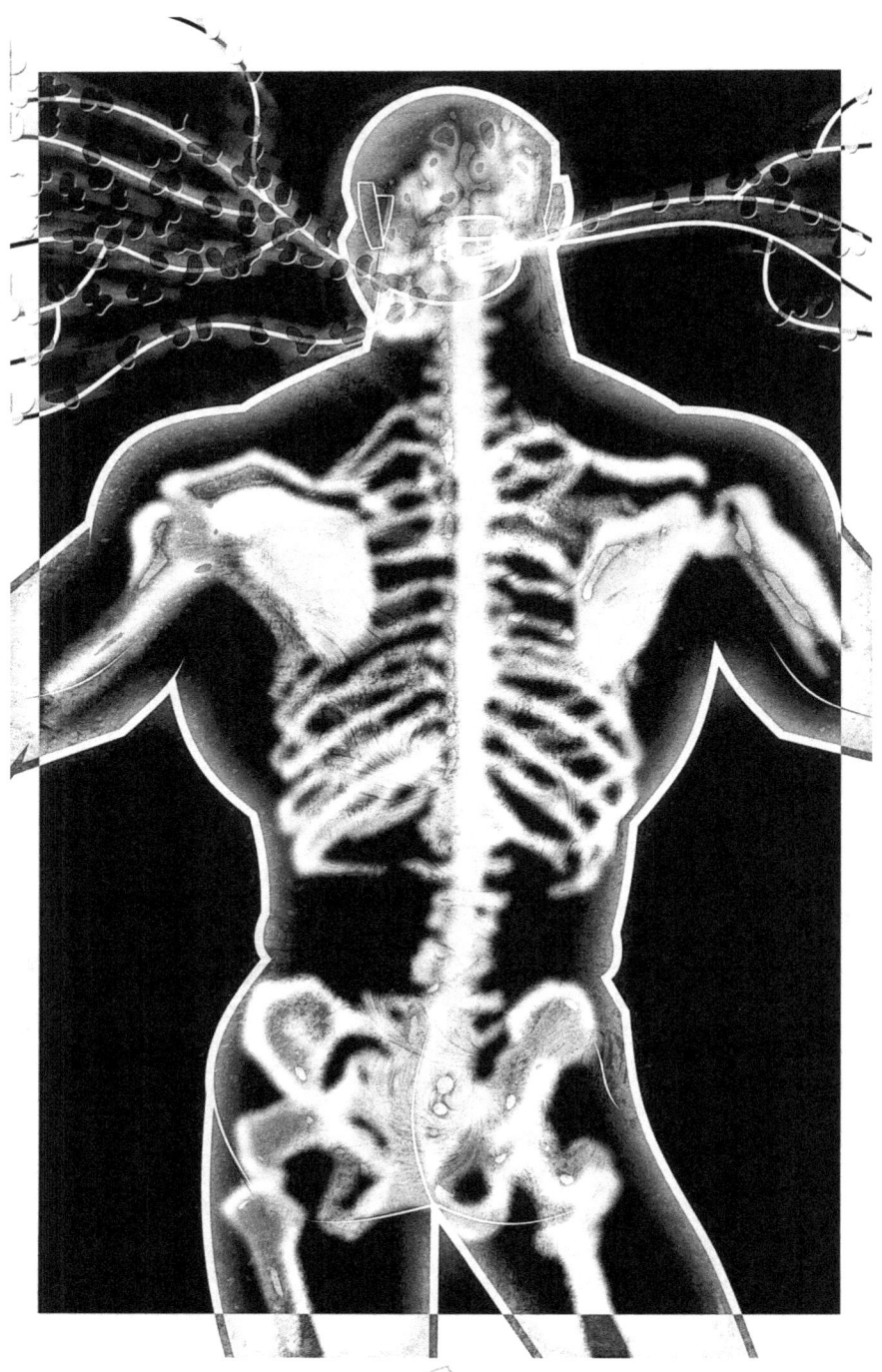

The Art of Balance

DISTANCE. Such a stretch across the waters of the globe from Australia to the U.S. A long, tedious flight back to the place Gael was born and grew up; the place he was trying to get some distance from. All he could think of was distance. Distancing himself from the pair of American idiots in the row in front of him, from the discomfort of his seat, from the peanut lodged between his teeth, from the education in Sydney he had to give up, and from the illness that was soon to be, he knew, the focal point of his existence. Everyone around him would remind him of it. This rare disease. A malformation of blood vessels strangling the nerves in his medulla.

He would distance himself from it all. Try and act indifferent. Like it wasn't happening. Certainly not happening to him. He would be a spectator, a witness to an attack on a body. Distance; yes, distance would help him. (*Stress and density.*) So even as he closed the gap between continents, another stretch and chasm was forming in his mind.

CAT rubbed Gael's back as Gael threw up his breakfast. The gagging afterwards was always worse. They would cause unstoppable tears to stream down his face. As soon as Cat helped him back to the bed the hiccups began. Gael moaned with despair. He could always tell when the hiccups were to start.

There was a sudden build up of force in his lungs and throat. As if everything had been closed up and then suddenly released.

"When is your next doctor's appointment?" Cat asked, trying to divert attention from the hiccups.

"Next week.... I hate them. They've already told me...they can't operate. They can't get at the...problem." Hiccups permeated Gael's speaking. "I have five of the damn things in...my head! Everyone's astonished by that. The one...causing the problem is at the base of my brain.... Nobody wants to touch it."

"Can you blame them? You don't want to be paralyzed." Cat now sat back beside the bed on the old wooden chair. His eyes looked as if he were on the verge of tears. There was something else in his eyes as well, Gael thought. Fear maybe? What was it? There was an inkling of some other emotion. Gael could not place it. Something untold.

"Every time I visit a doctor I...get my hopes up that somehow some miracle will happen.... They'll tell me that a new radical surgery can...fix me. That I'll be back to myself in no time but...." Gael hit the mattress in anger. "I hate these hiccups!" He calmed down again. "Hope is a curse."

"Don't give up." Cat put his hand on Gael's shoulder. "I don't know what else I can say."

Gael looked at Cat and smiled. "You're great.... You've been great. I'm just afraid of wasting...wasting time."

There was the truth. His mind went back to the year or so after his father had died. A year of complete loss. A breakdown and closing off. He thought to himself that he would never again see the summer the way he once had. Summer, going on just outside his bedroom walls, was lost to him forever. No more swimming pools, no more jogs at sunset, no more crickets at night, nothing. His self-pity had reached its zenith.

The despair had grown from depression. He wanted nothing but sleep. He certainly didn't want to be seen by anyone, especially Cat. But Cat would not let Gael be.

"You sleep too much." "Let me shave your face. You're looking a little shaggy." "I'm cutting your hair. Let's shave it. It'll be sexy." "I brought some new CDs. Let's give 'em a listen."

Cat would sit with Gael for hours. All the while Gael thought himself repulsive and wished for Cat to be gone, to leave. The first time that thought had ever come into Gael's mind.

Eventually, Cat succeeded in getting Gael up. They went out on the front porch on that first uneasy journey through the old house. It was a rainy pre-fall day in mid-September. Gael's mother brought him a quilt as he sat in a wicker chair. Cat sat on the porch swing opposite Gael.

"Stop looking at me. You're making me uncomfortable." The hiccups were absent for a bit.

"Sorry. I just want to be sure you're okay. You should get up like this every day. Take small steps. You can get better." Cat was almost pleading.

"I don't think so, Kitten." Gael looked out into the rain. He wanted to run out into it.

Cat sighed exasperated. "I don't know what to do. You've given up. You look awful! You're letting yourself waste away. You can't give up –"

"I can! I have! There's no point.... You don't know what it's like. Everything has been snatched away."

"You know, when you left for Australia I wished and hoped that something would happen. That something would stop you from going. Or bring you home." Cat was crying, looking out into the rain. "You've got to get better!" He stopped and wiped his nose with his hand. Cat rose to his feet and walked quickly off the porch to his car. Gael couldn't say anything.

Gael sat on the porch curled up in his mother's quilt watching the rain. There was a dip in the roof of the porch that allowed the rain to collect and overflow like a small waterfall. Gael focused on this, watching the water fall from the roof to the live-forevers below.

He heard a sniff from the screen door. His mother was standing there, eyes red from crying. *How long had she been there? Had she seen the argument?*

"What's wrong?" Gael asked, his eyes half closed from the heaviness of despair.

His mother sniffed. "I just hate seeing you like this," she said, and then walked away. It was enough, he thought. People were hurting because of his stubbornness. His inability to see past his own barriers. Things would have to change.

REHABILITATION came in the form of a clinic linked to the nearest hospital in Verona. Gael underwent both physical and occupational therapy. The staff was kind and not as harsh or demanding as he had envisioned them. In a week he noticed small improvements: he could move a finger on his right hand, stand for a few seconds without support, and bend his right wrist ever so slightly. The occupational therapist, a kind, older woman named Becca, was even teaching him to write left-handed. The physical therapist, a younger man named Ray, thought it a good idea for Gael to use a walker while he was learning to get on his feet again. So into Gael's life came Nelly the Walker. She was actually a steel cane with four feet at the base. Nelly was designed for his left hand more for steadying himself than actually walking with. Nelly was so called because whenever Gael would almost fall or need support he would jokingly exclaim "Whoa Nelly!" It made him laugh and seemed to lift the spirits of those around him as well. Therapy was three days a week, two hours a day. Gael hated it, but at the same time, knew the result of going could mean recovery.

When he could, Cat would come down and spend the day with Gael, taking him to his appointments. Gael liked this. He liked having Cat at therapy. Having him there meant that he couldn't slack off or take it easy. Cat expected Gael to break a sweat, to reach beyond.

"How's Nelly working out for you?" Cat asked once as he drove Gael to a therapy appointment.

"She's okay. Wish I didn't need her," Gael said, uninterested in the question and watching the leaves scatter along the road.

"You're somewhere else today, huh?" Cat interrupted Gael's thoughts. "You gonna work hard today?"

"I'll do what I can," Gael said, annoyed at the question. "It's not easy. I don't know how it looks, but it's not easy. I don't know why I'm doing all of this. Is it actually going to do any good?" Cat stayed quiet, letting Gael revel in a moment of self-pity.

Inside the clinic, Cat stayed by Gael as he went through his therapy. The day was devoted to working on balance. Side-stepping, stop-starts, walking on heels, standing on one leg, and trying stairs for the first time. The latter Gael did very well. Better than expected, Ray said. Across the large room Gael saw an old man. He was shuffling with a walker along the inside of the parallel bars. He wasn't getting very far, but he was determined to reach the end. Every time his therapist asked if he needed to have a seat, he would sternly answer in the negative. Ray saw Cat and Gael looking over at the older patient. "There's some inspiration for you," he said as Gael rested on a chair.

"What?" Gael replied.

Eric Arvin

"Mr. Grace. He's been here before," Ray said as he glanced over his shoulder. "He's recovering from his fifth stroke. Doctors are all amazed he's still alive, but he keeps coming back. He gets knocked down, and he just keeps getting up." Ray looked back at Gael. "Human will, huh?" He smiled. Gael looked up to see Cat staring at him and grinning.

"I get it, all right," Gael said. "You don't have to hit me over the head with it." Cat laughed. "And wipe that grin off your face," Gael said as he rose from his chair to have another go at the art of balance.

BY the time the spring pushed its way through the midwestern snows Gael was feeling much better. Everything showed signs of recovery. His walking had improved to the point that Nelly was no longer needed. There was a gait to his steps but only slight and hardly noticeable. His hiccups had disappeared months before, and the vertigo had subsided substantially. The last hold-outs were his fingers on his right hand. He could use his arm fine, but the fingers were still not gripping. His physical therapist told him his grip would be the last thing to return to use. In the meantime he was writing quite well with his left hand. Over time, other activities he had done with his right hand became more easily accomplished with his left. (He discovered the joys of masturbation anew.)

His condition, while slowing his life course down to the point of freeze, had also given him a certain awareness. In fact, he had *become* aware. Aware of things he had forgotten and overlooked. Lying in a bed for extended periods of time had let him see the world of his family more closely. To be sure, it was the same family he had struggled to get away from, but they had all changed. Changes he never really noticed until he was bedridden and all that was left to do was study the elements of the world around him.

He felt shame for missing out on certain things over the past few years. While he was at college he rarely came home, and every summer would find a reason to stay on campus. It wasn't that he hated his family; it was that some memories had a way of driving him away. When he would return to his mother's home, it seemed as if these memories screamed at him. They clung to the very walls of the house itself and battered him with blame and disappointment. As Gael was forced to remain in the house sick, though, the screaming voices became lessened, and then they weren't there any longer. Once he became more comfortable with his surroundings and less afraid of the past, he began to do things with his family. Board games, movies, make dinner, or simply stand around in the kitchen and talk.

SPRINGTIME offered more time for Gael and Cat to get together. Cat was able to arrange his hours, being only part time now, so that he could take care of the ailing Rosa and come see Gael as well. It felt good for Gael to workout again. To feel that high at the end of a session. He knew, of course, that he would never again be able to lift the 150-pound dumbbells, but that was okay. He had grown tired of the others in the gym competing with him in feats of strength. One-upmanship was something he could never understand in the arena of fitness. He only wanted to look good naked again. His grip may not have been strong, but the strength in his arm seemed not to diminish much during his illness

They often drove to their alma mater and sat on the sloping grass that overlooked the river. Barges passed below and student joggers passed just above them on the narrow paths of the campus.

"Thank you, Kitten," Gael said quietly while looking out on the river. He leaned back on his hands with his legs stretched out into the uncut grass. A sweet breeze passed up from the river.

"For what?" Cat looked at him puzzled.

"For being here. For doing all this. You've helped me out so much while I've been sick. I don't think I've shown you very much gratitude. Sometimes I think I've been mean, downright rude to you." He looked over at Cat. "Thanks for everything."

"It's no problem, man." Cat smiled. "I love being around you. Even when you look like shit," he laughed.

"But I haven't treated you as good as..." Gael went silent and looked to the grass, "...as good as you deserve."

"Hey stop," Cat said, putting his hand on Gael's leg. "Nobody can be blamed for being a little off when they are as sick as you were. I mean, everyone's allowed to be an asshole at some point." Gael laughed and pushed Cat down onto the grass.

"Is that why you drive so far to see me? Because you like being near me?" Gael asked.

"You bet," Cat said.

"That's nice," Gael replied staring back onto the water. "I like being near you too. *I like it a lot,*" he said in his best Forrest Gump voice. For a time, they sat in silence but for the breeze and songs of birds. "How is Rosa?" Gael asked.

"Better. She's gone into remission. The therapy seems to have worked."

"That's great. Maybe I should come visit her again."

Cat looked at him. "We'll see. She's still pretty religious. She might say something that'll offend you. In fact, I know she will. You're so easily offended."

"I don't know. I kinda get it now, you know, the whole religious thing." Gael paused. "Well, maybe not religion, but spirituality. I think I get it now."

"How's that, baby?" There was a funny look of fear spread across Cat's face.

"While I was sick, I mean really sick and depressed, all I could think of was death. I wanted to die sometimes. You know, I heard about this Native American tribe. Back yonder, in the days when they were being killed by the thousands, if one of this particular tribe was captured they would simply die. They saw no future. They had no *conception* of the future. They believed their current situation, being behind bars or in a camp, was how it was going to be forever. They couldn't deal with it, and so they would just die." Gael stopped. "I think I was like that. I couldn't see there was a future. Another future that I hadn't counted on. Different than the one I had designed in my head or from what I was in."

"How did you get out of that? Out of that way of thinking?"

Gael sighed and breathed in the fresh spring air. "I thought I was dying, you know, but I didn't want this life to be all there was. I like existing, you know, having a perspective." Cat nodded his head. "I started thinking of Heaven. What I would want it to be like, and I came up with my own interpretation of the afterlife, I guess. I think my heaven is everything I have ever loved. Everything I need. Heaven is made of the things that make you get warm goose bumps. Things that make your heart feel cleansed." He looked at Cat. "You think it's ridiculous, don't you? Corny?"

"I think it's a wonderful idea."

"Everything has a purpose. Everything has a reason. If I break a rubber band or break a leg, there's a reason for it. I think now that everything turns out the way it's supposed to." Gael didn't know if he *believed* any of what he was saying, but it sounded just as plausible as the things he had been forced to believe as a child.

"A divine plan? Do you believe in that? That some god has a plan for all of us? Every little, insignificant thing on the Earth?" Cat sounded incredulous.

"No, not a divine plan as such. Maybe just that things are already set in motion, and there's a way they go and no one can put a kink in the wheels. There's no fucking it up. Whatever is up there, God or the Force," Gael smiled at Cat, "has reasons for making things go as they do. I think I would have just died if I hadn't come up on that idea, on some idea. I asked God once to make me a better person. Maybe this is how he answered. I developed, am still developing, my own theology." He paused. "And *nothing* is insignificant, Cat."

"I guess having your own theology is better than having blind faith in some of the shit they serve you at these churches," Cat said. "But if it was God who made you feel like you did and get that sick, I think he's a total dick."

GAEL felt alive again. Like a great wind had been blown into his body, rushing down veins and pipes and through organs, making everything crisper, newer. He felt new at releasing his infant theology into the world. As if saying it loud gave it credence, made it substantial and true. He massaged his head and breathed in deeply the pristine spring air. Instead of returning home, Gael decided he would go with Cat to his apartment in the city. There, he would apply to another school starting the following September. It would be a new start. Fresh. And there would be no plans made. No plans for a future he could never control.

At night, Gael lay in the comfort of Cat's arms again and enjoyed the carnality of sex. It had been a while. The gift that was the pleasure of flesh had never felt so intense. Passionate, animalistic, aware. He felt he had new senses, or at least sharper, more tuned old ones. Everything was bright and clean and the way it was supposed to be by design. Cat made Gael feel sexy even if Gael wasn't in top form yet. The ball player still knew how to swing. Cat kissed Gael hard, as if he were starved. He played with Gael's body like it was the first time, except with a more intense curiosity. (Gael was sure there would be a purple bruise when Cat bit hard on his nipple making him scream just a little.) They continued rough and riding through the night until exhaustion overtook them. Finally, Gael laid his head on Cat's stomach and traced the butterfly tattoo on his inner thigh. Everything was good. Everything had purpose.

Eric Arvin

An Ordinary Evening,
An Ordinary Couple

IT was September and the first week of my return to education —
in the scholastic sense anyway. Autumn would come soon. My
things and I had been moved to Cat's new apartment. Having my
things in his apartment was advantageous to him. The furniture
and other items I had collected over the years filled up his empty
spaces well. He was not one for furniture shopping, nor for any
shopping for that matter. He thought it tedious. But, upon
moving my things in, I could see on his face a certain satisfaction.
A relief maybe of seeing the apartment come to life. Finally. My
old coffee table that had wasted so many years in the garage was
the first thing moved in. It replaced the milk crates covered by
plywood that had served as Cat's own makeshift table. The coffee
table took up a great amount of room. Cat immediately took to it,
though. He fixed the stout little legs so that they no longer
wobbled, then put his feet up on it, sat back, and turned on
ESPN2. I was pleased to see the table used at last.

Thursday night of my first week there, the apartment
possessed the tone of quiet and fatigue. The lights were dimmed,
and the city shone in from the bay window that overlooked the
street. Nick Drake's *Five Leaves Left* played quietly.

We sat on the couch in the living area of the apartment
eating a mish-mash of leftovers I had found in his fridge. Rice,

cheese, tuna, sweet and sour chicken, and tomatoes mixed with an assortment of spices. Cat named it Mutt 'n' Slop. We both had heaping portions since we had not eaten all day. I ate furiously. Cross-legged and slumped over my bowl like someone was about to steal it away. I dropped the spoon a few times, for my grip was still a little less than strong. Cat sat comfortably with his legs on the coffee table, crossed at the ankles. I loved seeing him like that. Totally at ease, with no shirt and loose-fitting pajama bottoms.

"Food good," Cat groaned in his most caveman-ish huff, shoveling in a huge portion of the slop. He reached over and rubbed my head which had been freshly shaven. He liked the feel of my naked scalp, so I kept the look for him. Though, at times, I did miss my hair, I loved the feel of his hands massaging my head. It was the closest thing to orgasm there was, but without all the work before and the mess after. I would never have thought of shaving my hair off before Cat mentioned it, but he was always a convincing addiction for me. I would usually end up doing what he wanted. And he was usually right about things. In the summer, as I was regaining my strength, I had even succumbed to his recommendation that I get a tattoo to celebrate my triumph over illness. I decided on a four-leaf clover in that sexy area right below the waist on the hip; the cum-gutter, he so eloquently referred to it.

"How's the new gig?" I asked as I slurped up the last of my Mutt 'n' Slop.

"I like it a little better," Cat said as he put his bowl down on the coffee table. His new job was in an insurance agency. It wasn't his dream, but the pay was good, and he thought it at least a step up from selling clothes to bitchy teenagers at the GAP. Yet, already it had induced its share of eyebrow pulling. "When I can, I would like to get back to school. I don't know what for, though. I can't think of a thing I'd want to do."

"You've got a business degree. You could become a lawyer. Fight for gay rights," I said, half serious.

"Gael, I can't even come out to my own mother. You can't then expect me to be a rectifier of gay problems to the public." Yet, in his eyes, I could definitely see a spark of interest. I shrugged.

"Speaking of your mother, how is she?"

"Everything is good right now. She says she has more good days than bad days. All of her churchy friends are keeping her spirits up. I suppose they're good for that, anyway. She looks much better. Her hair is finally coming back." He stared blankly across the room at the turned off television.

"She looked great when I saw her, Kitten," I said, trying to dissuade his thoughts from entering darker territories. "She looked very well." I smiled. His eyes caught mine.

"She does," he whispered, more as a reassurance to himself than a response to me. "She was strong, wasn't she, helping us move in? Gotta be honest. I was a little worried that she might catch on...."

"Catch on? Oh. Catch on to the fact that there is only one bed, and we fuck in it?" I grinned wildly and leaned over to twist his nipple.

"Gael!" Cat laughed, swatting my hand away.

"Baby, I think she might suspect already. Mothers have a sixth sense about their lil' gay boys." I was trying to make him smile more. He reached over and gave *my* right nipple a hard twist. "Yowch!" I hollered, "that hurt!" Cat just snickered.

"How are classes?" Cat asked, changing the course of conversation. Nick Drake crooned on in the background.

"Fine. It's just like when I was studying in Oz, though. I've already been through most the books. Verona was a good school, it turns out. It prepared us well."

"How do you feel physically? Are you getting around okay?"

"Eh," I shrugged. The truth was my leg bothered me from time to time, and my vertigo was ever-present in small amounts. Since my grip hadn't completely returned, I was also still having problems writing with my right hand. None of this I told him, though. Thinking about Rosa was all the worry I could bear to watch him suffer through, and that was difficult.

"I talked to Evan on instant messenger today in between classes," I said, again changing the course of the conversation. "She says hi."

"Does she?" Cat replied doubtfully.

"She doesn't hate you, Cat." I was maybe a little too emphatic on this point. In truth, she hadn't said hi at all. And while she didn't exactly say she hated Cat....

Excerpt from an on-line conversation between Gael and Evan:

Heavenlyevan34 says: Are you and the ball-playing closet case still together?

Gaelofverona says: Yes, Evan, darling, we're very happily together.

Heavenlyevan34 says: He's a shit! I'm sorry but I really don't like him.

"She's getting married. That guy we met in Australia, Liam, well, he asked her to marry him," I said.

"Thaaaat's greeeat," Cat said dryly and without exclamation. "Does that mean she'll be out of our life and back to Oz?" He grinned as he said this.

"I don't know, but we *are* going to the wedding," I assured him and brought my point home with a severe look.

"Ah, shitcrackers!" He grabbed a pillow from the couch and smothered it over his face. "All right," he said, putting the pillow down, "I'm going to bed. You coming?"

"I'll be there in a while. I'm going for seconds," I said as we both rose from the couch. "Remember," I yelled at him as he walked off toward the bedroom, his bubble booty swinging away beneath the thin material of his pajama bottoms, "fifty push ups before bed."

A Massacre of Lions

THE coldest bitter winds of a mid-January freeze could never compare to the feel of a hospital's bleak aura. The very air seems frigid and hung with invisible icicles that chime desperation as the doctors and visitors pass through them. Avoidance of such places was a life ambition for me. Yet, it *was* January, and there we were, Cat and I, at the hospital. Rosa had fallen ill again, very ill. She was laid up and given what comfort could be offered to her. In such cases "comfort" becomes an empty word.

"There's nothing more that can be done," the doctor whispered to Cat in that ominous medical way. Rosa would suffer in her last days.

Cat was stone for most of the morning. Paralyzed by a form of grief, madness, and nostalgia. Whispers of seemingly unimportant moments he had spent with his mother haunted him, and he wished them all back. Still, I knew that it would be the suffering that would undo his emotions. Eventually he would crumble and sob. It was coming, this breakdown, *but when*? When would the stone facade crack?

Cat sat beside his mother on the bed. The unpassionate rhythm of varied hospital equipment droned around us in low worrisome meters. Rosa had been sleeping, but was awake again. The pain of her disease was lessened a little by drugs being pumped into her system continuously. The room was private. One of the rooms on the top floors of the hospital given to the terminally ill to allow them to springboard to Heaven. The blinds had been drawn back so she could see out onto the retreating world. Revealed was the icy metropolis creeping out to a far horizon. It was a desolate sight. One not worthy of her last view of the earth. A sudden spring or an Indian summer would have been more appropriate; more adherent to the rules of poetry and what we all dream our last days to resemble.

Rosa's hair was thinned, and her skin looked delicate and painfully transparent. Her flesh clung to her bones like wet clothes, and her eyes were clouded by drugs and fatigue. Cat tried comforting her with pillows. That was all he knew to do. Anything else was too labored with thought for that aching moment. He was as pale as the sheets she lay on, but as rigid as the bed rails at her side. Never had he experienced death like this. A hopeless drifting away. The intensity was overwhelming for him, and there was nothing I could say. No soothing words. To say it was all going to be all right was a mean and spiteful stab with an overused cliché. When Rosa would moan Cat knew it was never, ever going to be okay.

"This getting sick, this growing old," Rosa whispered to both of us, "it's vindictiveness. It's our bodies getting back at us for everything we've forced them to do." She smiled at me. "You should be wearing a hat, Gael," she pointed to my shaved head; something I had taken to doing for convenience. "You'll be in a hospital with pneumonia before you know it." Her voice, which had always been a robust instrument, was now only a shadow of an echo.

"I told him before we left to grab something for his head," Cat interjected, still looking dazed. He could have been unaware he had even put thought to words, such was his facial expression.

"You listen to Cat. He'll take good care of you."

My eyes darted from Rosa to Cat in surprise. *Had he at last told her the truth? That we were lovers?*

Rosa mumbled something to herself as she broke her gaze from me to look out the window. She seemed to be drifting off but then soon turned to us again. "It's a tragedy," she whispered.

"What is, Mom?" Cat asked.

"Getting sick. Even if it *doesn't* kill you it's a bloody tragedy. Some things you went into the illness with don't come out with you at the end. They get massacred. Slashed away and hacked at until a person can't hold onto them any longer. Certain ideals, ideals I proudly believed in, are gone forever. I can never trust in some of those things again. It's like a massacre... a massacre of lions. Ideas I thought were at the core of who I was. Ideas I believed I gained strength from." She was slow and wistful, pronouncing every word and syllable precisely. "I've spent my whole life following rules," Rosa said, trailing off into her own thoughts. "They were everyone else's rules. Never mine. *And still*, I accepted them because I was told to." She looked lost. Suddenly, she raised her fist and her voice in a revolt against disease. "I am sick to death of learning everyone's lessons! I wish now I had some to give of my own. I wish...." A look of concern came over her face. "I think I was wrong to have followed the path I did. I should have been freer. Religion told me to think certain ways...and I did without question. Don't get me wrong, Cat. I still believe in God. But religion, as such, is so divisive. I've decided that...just now. It tears the world apart. It seeks to put a strict structure to faith and spirituality where none should exist." She grabbed Cat's hand and squeezed with what strength she had left. "Faith should not have structure. It's a wild thing," she said with verve. "It's free and inquisitive; a whirling idea that flails akimbo." She looked into her son's face; tears threatened the edges of her dulled eyes.

Cat stroked his mother's thinned hair. "It's all right, Mom," he hushed her as he swallowed the lump in his throat.

"Live your life, boys," she said, looking earnestly at me now. "Don't you dare follow any other guides other than that which is pulling you. Don't let anyone convince you that your belief system is any less than theirs."

She looked over to the table by her bed. Her Bible lay open on it. Someone had been reading to her; a night nurse or a preacher. "Cat, darling, hand me that, please," she said fraily. Cat reached over and picked up the heavy book. "This is a good book." She paused. "I know your feelings on it, Cat, but it has worth. There are good lessons for living. But you know what the main theme of this book is? It's simple. *God is love*. That's it. If people stopped and simply took that in.... But they don't. They scrape away at these great stories. Sculpting their own hateful theories and dangerous notions. It turns from something so beautiful to an angry work of isolation." She grasped the Bible with both hands as firmly as she could. "*God is love*. Remember that every time you feel unsure about your life and its turns. Don't let the morality thumpers eat at you. How dare they decide your morals from their strangled interpretations! *They have no right!*" She had tried to yell this last bit, but it only came out as a harsh whisper. Cat stared up at me, his eyes straining to keep back tears.

"Are you all right, Rosa? Do you need a nurse?" I asked, coming nearer to her.

"No...no, I'm fine." She loosened up again. With gentle eyes she looked at me. "I want you to have this." She stretched out her frail arms to give the leather Bible to me, and I accepted it gently. "I have marked some passages for you."

Sure enough, a long silk red ribbon marked a place in the book so that a strand of it hung loosely from either side of the closed volume of ancient stories.

"Do you know," she said as I glided my fingers across the Bible in my hands, "the Hebrew word *ahbh,* meaning love, is translated as love in the context of sexual desire."

Cat smiled a little. He had never heard his mother talk of such things.

"It's used all throughout the Bible," she said.

Cat and I were puzzled. What was this? *Ahbh*? Was she remembering a past sermon at church? She was definitely dozing off. Her mind was wandering, we thought. Grabbing memories from a life's slideshow.

We stayed a while longer. It felt as if we were in a tomb. The sound of hospitals is very tomblike after all. Echoes layered upon echoes laid over hushes and sobs. I sat down at the end of Rosa's bed until Cat was prepared to leave. Rosa slept peacefully at last, and Cat kissed her on the forehead as we readied ourselves for the journey home.

"IT'S the story of David and Jonathan," I said as I opened the Bible to the passages Rosa had marked.

We were on the interstate headed back to our apartment. Cat drove with zombie-like efficiency through the maze of other vehicles. His mind was still back with Rosa, but his body knew the way home fine by itself. The gray and cloudy silhouette of the city mumbled past us. It seemed uninhabitable, this ugly cold city of steel.

"The book of 1 Samuel. She has marked 18:1-3 and 20:41," I explained.

"Read it to me," Cat said. They were the first words he had spoken since we left the hospital. His eyes were still staring ahead, emotionless.

I began:

"*And it came about that, as soon as he had finished speaking to Saul, Jonathan's very soul became bound up with the soul of David, and Jonathan began to love him as his own soul....*

And Jonathan and David proceeded to conclude a covenant, because of his loving him as his own soul."

I stopped and looked up.

"Keep reading," Cat said, his voice cracking.

"Chapter 20, verse 41. She has this underlined:

...and they began kissing each other and weeping for each other, until David had done it the most.

"There's a note to the side that says 2 Samuel 1:26." I turned quickly to the passage and began to read:

"I am distressed over you, my brother Jonathan. Very pleasant you were to me. More wonderful was your love to me than the love from women."

There was a word written in the margin here as well. "Ahbh," I whispered completely moved. "She's written it here beside the passage." There was also written something else that I did not read to Cat.

Take care of him, Rosa had scrawled shakily.

"Cat..." I choked out. My heart was breaking.

"She knows," he said as his words took on the sound of collapse. It was time. He quickly pulled to the shoulder of the interstate and put the car in park. I waited for a howl; a loud thunderous moan. Slowly, the emotion welled up in him like lava and ash making its way out from the top of a great mountain.

It poured from him, all the tears and hurt and anger. He hit and yelled and threw the fit I knew had been set to come. The car filled with his curses. At last, I grabbed him, his whole body fighting me and shaking. He was wet from tears as he finally succumbed to grief over anger and collapsed fully into me. I held him there. The grey city towered over; its uncaring denizens rushing past us.

*   *   *

Rosalind (Rosa) Allyson Strong passed on January 29, 2004, after a long illness. A lifelong resident of the state, she was an active member of St. John's Sixth Street Church. She gave of herself willingly. An avid supporter of literacy, her favorite book was *O Pioneers!* She is survived by a son, Michael Cather Strong. A memorial service to be held at St. John's, 11:00. Interment at Everhome Cemetery.

Eric Arvin

As Told by Lamarr Robert Irving...

IN life I was a simple man. A simple man who used simple words and relied upon the most obvious and apparent conclusions and descriptions that were handed to me. There were no mysteries other than those my god, Jehovah, wished to remain as such. Being among the simple men, I was laid to rest, as they that do the laying like to refer to it, under a simple stone plaque on the earth. The stone read my name, dates of birth and death, and, as it was paid for by the government, my military service. Beside my name was carved a crucifix, a cross. Certainly a cross on my stone was nothing I would have wanted if asked in life. I wanted no part of what I used to refer to as 'worldly religions.' My family knew this. They knew my adamant devotion to my religion. A religion that did not believe Christ was put to death on a cross. So over the carved idol of the cross, that representation of another faith's Christ, my newly widowed wife adhered, by cement paste, a broach-like portrait of a young and smiling me, Lamarr Robert Irving.

I was born into the world on July 31, 1942, in the midst of the great upheaval of the second World War. My mother named me Lamarr after an actress, Hedy Lamarr. The irony is I never cared for movies. I only saw a few in my entire life and was never much impressed by them. Robert was my father's name. My mother died a year after I was born due to complications brought on by my birth. This left my father with a space in his heart he was only able to fill, it seemed, with liquor. He never married again. Nor did he ever show me any affection until the day he fell off a ladder while painting his barn and died on the paint speckled ground below. I spent the next few years in the care of my aunt. It was not a comfortable arrangement for either of us. We were more strangers than family. She, like my father, was a hard drinker and had many male friends. I never finished high school and joined the army as soon as I was of age. This got me away from my aunt and out on my own. I was sent all over the world and the traveling suited me. When I tired of the life, however, I returned and met my future wife while she waited tables at a roadside diner. In three weeks we were engaged to be married. The rest of my life was ordinary in most respects. I found a job that paid well and began to raise a family in a little house in this stoic, somewhat stagnant river valley. I became a Jehovah's Witness and tried to rear my family in that faith. The children — Javon, Trent, Gael, and Ella — were the light of my life. 'Light' being a more appropriate word than you can probably believe right now. I did, in my time on earth, try for better things. Possibly to make them proud. I built a garage in hopes of opening my own business with a partner but, in the end, it was not to be. So I let the dream die and tried my best to forgive the man who had left me with the debt. After a lifetime of working, many joys, and some great disappointments, one morning in a grey hospital bed, I passed out of the world I had known and into the great warm bask of the light that waits.

In my mid-fifties, hardly an old man, my body had finally given in to rest and peace. I was buried in Verona.

It was Gael who, it seems, took the longest route in adjusting. Indeed, he had no focus, only ideas of a controllable future; a destiny by his own design. He dreamt of big rooms. At least one large enough for an old dust green coffee table which served as an anchor for a life away from what he had known. And he collected books. Volumes of works to fill his shelves. Books from school and shops. *The Complete Works of William Shakespeare; Dante's Inferno; Mama Day; The Decameron; The*

Age of Constantine the Great; Herodotus; Plutarch's Lives; The Malleus Malificarum; City of God; Euripides. It was all very academic and impressive, but it lacked anything else. For him, there was certainly no road to fulfillment to be found in all those pages. His light was a rigid blue streak that hardly wavered.

Before I died, Gael longed to leave Verona; to get out for good. After I died, he felt only blame and self-loathing. He spent a time in utter silence from the world. He was drawn away by his own inner turmoil. Pulling himself from this, he became concerned, constantly eaten up, by the idea of lost time. A wasted life. He saw time as a great enemy. He did not understand that there is no such thing as wasted time, nor of a wasted life. It all goes on as it should. His illness, a thing I surely would have felt an enormous amount of guilt for if I were living, only added to his disparaging ideas on the flow of his existence. Yet, he came from it with a new outlook. A surprisingly spiritual one. His light grew and grows still. His adjustment to sorrow, to loss, was a shaky one. It seemed, though, that he grew through his adversity. Done what we are all supposed to do in dire situations. Take from it and grow. Let those around us who needed it feel our light. And Gael's light was needed to shine on one close to him. Another who had felt the stabbing human pain of loss. His friend, his lover, and soul-partner Cat.

After a span of years, nearly ten by Gael's count, it was finally time for him to visit the place where my ashes were buried. There was no poetic scattering of my remains in a river or over a high hill. I was simply put under the earth beneath a grave marker. A silly idea, a grave marker, really. Relatives and friends return year after year and visit a plot of land that, in truth, holds nothing of the person they once loved and knew. There is nothing of the soul left there. There are no meandering ghosts or spirits milling about and watching over their sullen, depressing graves. It is in no way the resting place that everyone is told it is. What a dreadful thought, to lie in one spot with the soul leashed there for all time! Its simple purpose, though, is an important one. It offers closure and comfort to those left behind. And thus it did for Gael.

Gael's reason given for coming was that he wanted to inspect the picture, that of my young face, that was cemented to the stone marker. It had been knocked from its place, now its second time. The cross showed where the photo had been. The family suspected something sinister. Vandalism by teenagers. This was not the case. The keepers of the stone garden were simply mowing over the flat markers, and a blade had caught the picture, ripping it from its position. The truth behind this cover story of Gael's was that he had summoned up the courage to finally find peace. He thought it an appropriate day to find this peace, this closure. It was his birthday. It was spring.

There was no jumping right into it, though. Gael did not directly make a line for the grave marker bearing my name. He eased into it, taking a slow and nervous promenade through the large cemetery that lay at the base of a bluff overlooking the valley. They began reading the more ancient stones near the rocky wall and wistful trees at the edge of the garden. This was at the very side of the bluff directly opposite of my marker. The dates on these stones went back centuries. These were the stones that were moved, along with the remains that could be found, after a great surge from the river flooded the town, forcing a reconstruction of the entire map of the world. At least, of the world to those in old Verona. Some of the markings were barely legible. Some had no markings at all. Some were crumbling and invaded by the roots of trees. Some were only small stones placed in the ground; markers for lost babies and children. Further away from the bluff wall there were more elaborate death markers. Great carved angels and other statuary loomed over the more simple stones around them. These in particular made Gael uneasy. They didn't seem comforting at all, but menacing. As if they could suck the life from the living, and indeed, some of the ground surrounding them was bare and dead-looking. Cat thought these huge stone monuments were a terrible waste of money.

As they approached closer to the spot where my ashes had been placed, Gael's steps grew slower. The pit of his stomach rumbled. A slight trembling overtook him. He tried to tame this feeling; replace it with a joke. He tried to calm his thoughts and emotions. "Feels like a movie out here today," he said to Cat, his fear masked with effort by a jovial tone.

"A movie?" Cat puzzled as he looked to the overcast sky. It had been breezy all day and cooler. It looked more autumn than spring. The trees had yet to fully dress themselves in their greenery. "How's that?" he asked, looking back to Gael.

"The feel of the day. It reminds me of *Ordinary People*. Did you ever see that movie?" Gael nervously rattled on. Cat shrugged. "There's a scene when Mary Tyler Moore is talking to Timothy Hutton in the backyard of their home. Today reminds me of that scene." Gael was smiling as he said this. It was a weak smile. Barely hanging on to the corners of his mouth. It escaped completely from his face as they approached my marker. He wondered how they had come to it so quickly. It had snuck up on him. Moved from one side of the garden to the next. It seemed to Gael that the stone marker had found its way over to him rather than the other way around.

As he stared at the name on the stone, and the dates, memories flooded his mind. In his hand, wrapped in paper towel, he grasped the picture he had planned to reattach. Sights and faces and words ran through his mind as a film. A badly edited one. He remembered arguments and laughter. He struggled to keep the bad times from his mind, but, as always happens, the terrible things are sometimes the only things people end up focusing on. His mind dwelt momentarily on a tree covered in snow and ice. Then on a memory of my face as Javon walked out the door long ago. And desperate, sad hallways of a hospital on a wintry morning. Finally, he focused on an idea, a thought. The gnawing pain that he was not there the morning I left the world. He did not come in to the room even once before I passed away. He had no final view of my face before the moment of death. He was back in Verona at that particular moment, though I saw him. At a moment when I rose from it all and saw the Great Net, the true connecting that joins us all, I perceived Gael by a window taking in his view the ice tree. Soon after he was told I had passed, and the guilt set in wholly. And that razor-toothed badger of guilt ate at him still. It was, however, loosening its grip. Closure is never really that which it claims. Nothing ever offers complete closure. But to forgive anything, mostly oneself, is the great exhale of held breath. That was what Gael searched for.

He stood gazing at the stone. 'Lamarr.' My lovely wife always called me by this name whenever she was irritated with me. Most of the time it was 'Daddy' and I referred to her as 'Mother.' Cat's hand rested on Gael's shoulder. He rubbed it tenderly. Gael did feel queasy, but he didn't break down in great sobs as he thought he would. It was more akin to shock that he felt at the moment. He simply stood in an almost dream-like clarity of the event he was a part of. He took in a deep breath. "Such a simple stone," he said to himself. "You know," he said to Cat, taking on that false bravado once more, "I think when I die I want something funny on my stone. I saw one once that made me laugh right there in the middle of the cemetery. Imagine...right in the middle of the cemetery. It said 'I told you I was sick!" He forced a quiet chuckle. Cat squeezed him closer. Gael frowned and rested his head on Cat's shoulder. A strong breeze whipped around them. Gael reached up and grabbed off the wool toboggan that covered his shaved crown.

Gael lowered himself, sitting cross-legged on the soft, fresh grass. Cat came down beside him. "How did you do it, Cat? How did you get yourself to go and visit Rosa so soon after she died? Where was that courage with me?" Gael was visibly concerned.

"It isn't about courage. I think it's more a thing of need. I wasn't ready, though I had plenty of warning. I know it wasn't a sudden thing, her death, but I still wasn't ready. I still needed to be near her. As for you and your dad, I think there were other issues." Cat looked at Gael. "This was the right time for you. Any earlier and...who knows?"

"Maybe so, but still I wish I had had the strength to be like you. To face things like you do." A slight chill ran over his body as a breeze caressed his head.

"Maybe I should have stayed away from her grave a bit longer," Cat said.

"Why?" Gael stared at him, disbelieving if he meant what he had said.

"You were there. The aftermath. Everything that happened those few weeks after Mom died. Maybe I wouldn't have gone through that if I hadn't so quickly faced up to the reality that she was gone. That she was buried in the ground underneath." Cat's voice cracked. After Rosa had died, and after the first visit to the grave, Cat had indeed gone into a downward spiral. A depressive state that Gael knew very well. So, Gael felt it was his turn to comfort and look after Cat as Cat had done for him while he was sick. It was a difficult few weeks. There were times when Cat refused to rise from bed altogether. He lay with thick covers pulled over his head. After all, he had lost the only woman he had ever loved, his mother. There were nights of bad dreams when Cat would wake hitting at the air and yelling, then burst into tears. A slight madness, it seemed to Gael. A sort of delirium had eased its way into Cat's everyday life. There were times in those days that Cat would be talking to the air as if it were Rosa. Gael would watch worried and misty-eyed from behind. The only thing he realized he could do for Cat was help him ride the pain out and keep him from slipping into despair. The sucking despair that Gael had known now twice in his life. It was a deep chasm that Gael did not want Cat to become acquainted with. In the end, after long nights of holdings following nightmares, mornings of forcing Cat from his bed, and days of keeping him from hard alcohol, light finally prevailed. Though, the sunlight would never shine the same again for Cat. Gael sensed this. There was a distance now that had wedged itself between Cat and everything around him. Something which Cat alone could repair. But would he even try? Gael's stomach had been twisted in knots over his lover.

The two of them sat cross-legged a while longer in the utter silence of the overcast morn. The wind was the only voice they heard. "Oh! I almost forgot. I brought you something." Cat reached into his pocket and pulled from it a piece of paper that had been folded and folded again. "I thought one day you might want this. It might at some point become meaningful for you." He handed the folded paper to Gael.

Gael opened the paper, almost ripping it, so creased and used it had become. It looked as if it had been looked at and handled time and again like a valuable old map or a favorite love letter. Gael's eyes widened as he began to read the top line: "*Autumn Jazz and Dad.*" He looked up at Cat, astonished. "Where did you get this? I thought I had lost it!"

"You actually threw it away. I picked it out of the trash and kept it for you. I only just recently found it when I was going through my school things cleaning out Mom's house. When you mentioned coming here on your birthday I thought it would be fitting." Cat's voice was light. Almost breathy.

Gael took a gulp. "Thank you," he whispered as he leaned toward Cat and kissed him softly on the cheek.

"You should read it. Here and now, and read it loud," Cat said as he smiled and his voice took on a sound of importance. Gael stared for a moment into Cat's eyes. Yes, it was sentimental.

"So this is *that* scene," Gael smiled as he looked back to the paper that was being tugged in his fingers by the breeze. "I'll play the part," he said, and then he began to read:

"The taste and smell of memory (breathe deep and speak)...."

He read it loud as Cat had told him to. His voice never quavered. It was at the end that the great scene finally unearthed him. He began to sob as he imagined he would. In those sobs, in the reading, in between and all about that moment, his guilt and worry were assuaged enough. Just enough. The act of creation is, in fact, the closest we ever come to God or true spirituality in our days of human existence. In this act there is hope. When one revisits something they had a hand in the creation of, they are reaffirming their own divinity. There is healing in that....

"...and silence is *so* accurate."

He leaned over to Cat who hung his arm around Gael's neck. After the tears, dried by hand and by breeze, they stood again towering over the small marker. "I feel so Sally Field," Gael said. They both laughed. Gael bent and picked up the picture wrapped in paper towel he had laid on the grass as he sat. Unwrapping it from its packaging, he stared at the photo. Cat went to the jeep to get the small mix of cement they had mixed before they came. So it was done simply and soon. The mixture was spread over the cross, and my photo was pressed firmly to the marker. "All better now," Gael sighed.

Gael and Cat turned and walked back to the jeep. "It was a good day," Gael said as they made their way from the cemetery and out onto the main highway. He sighed. In that sigh there was a promise. A promise to come and visit more often. To not let such an amount of time to pass before he would see me again. But then, there was no need for such a promise. I was with him and would ever be so. We are not tied to these old stone graves. "Let's go see Rosa," Gael said.

A Hat on the Bed

DURING the spring, the eve of Cat's departure for the navy finally arrived. There was a lump lodged uncomfortably in my throat all week. I kept my peace, however. I had given up in my quest to keep him to myself. His resolve stifled any stubborn anger I possessed. I knew he had to go. I knew there were things he needed to sort out away from those who knew him well.

We cleared the apartment, he in a frantic type of elation, me with a supportive, if strained, smile.

After talking it over it was decided that as soon as Cat left I would move from the apartment, our cozy second-floor dwelling with the bay window on Clay Street. When Cat came home on leave, he would find me in a new apartment at a university to the east. I had been offered a research position in the university history department.

We had begun packing and clearing things out a week earlier, and by our last night together we had only the essentials for a night's stay: the TV (sans cable), a mattress on the floor, toiletries, CDs and CD player, and some clothes.

There were only a couple of boxes of personal things that he wanted me to store in my father's garage until he returned. Cat wasn't materialistic. Among those treasures were baseballs signed with scribbles, athletic honors, a few photos, a framed picture of his mother Rosa, a few DVDs (*Field of Dreams* most definitely included). There were even a couple of books, though they were in no way to be considered high literature. Mostly they involved sport themes, baseball statistics and the like. There were some books about gay athletes like Dave Kopay and Billy Bean, and at the bottom of the pile there was the copy of *The Natural* by Bernard Malamud that I had bought him the previous Christmas.

Aside from the two boxes, there was nothing else he wanted to keep. Everything else would be sold or given to Goodwill or thrown away.

Most of his clothes – those that he wasn't taking with him – he set away for the needy, but I stole a few items I liked to see him strut about in and put them in with his other boxed items.

One article of clothing in particular I kept out and slipped on, a baseball jersey from our alma mater Verona College. The material felt soft due to countless turns in the wash, and it retained his smell – that essence of sweet onions. I breathed him in. A sentimental gesture, but it was, after all, a sentimental time. Cat smiled at me and continued working.

"When's the food get here? I'm starving," Cat said, waking me from my melancholy trance. We had been clearing things away all day and had not eaten. It was early evening, and every moment was one less in my contented little life.

"Should be here anytime," I replied, trying to sound not so glum.

"Here's the rest of the outfit," Cat said, gesturing to the jersey I was wearing. He held his Verona College baseball cap.

There was a knock at the door (our bell was broken), and I went to get the food. As I returned to Cat, I passed the mattress we had slept on the previous night. I might as well have just dropped the bags of Chinese food, I set them so harshly on the floor.

"Cat! What are you doing?" I yelled, as I snatched up the baseball cap he had thrown on the mattress.

He turned to me, wide-eyed and startled. "What the hell is wrong?" he yelled back.

"Don't put a hat on a bed," I said, still in horror. "It means someone's gonna die!"

"You're insane," Cat said.

"Cat, there's a war going on." I was trying to explain without breaking down completely. "And you're going to be in it. Don't you see? I'm not taking any chances...and neither should you."

He smiled and took the cap from my hand, putting it on my head. "Wear it, then."

"Looks good on you." He kissed me tenderly. "Hat on the bed! Where do you hear crazy shit like that?"

We ate our dinner as the hungry young men we were. It should have been a romantic thing, our last meal together. Instead it more resembled two pigs at their troughs as we sloppily slurped up the noodles.

It was in the shower that our night truly began. I loved washing him. Drawing the cloth and my bare hands over his body. Washing the hard muscles with care. I paid special attention to those regions which I knew would bring the most pleasure to him, and those I was particularly fond of myself – the surgical scar on his shoulder, the butterfly tattoo on his inner thigh. It would be the last time I would be able to do this for a while. I wanted it to last.

When the soaping was done, we stood and embraced, letting the warm water wash away any thoughts. This was the best feeling. Having him close like this. His wet, warm body pressed firmly against me. His arms wrapped securely around my back. His stiff penis pressed against my abdomen. My fingers squeezed his round ass cheeks. I would never be ready to let go.

Afterward, we at last tumbled to the mattress and a night of true love-making began. Not fucking, but love-making. In love, I opened myself up to him, and he to me. There were times during the night I wanted to cry. How could he be leaving me?

It was in the very early morning that we took a rest. He would need to sleep soon. His flight out was at ten that morning.

"If I had a cigarette I'd smoke it," Cat said, as he lay back on the mattress.

He glanced over at me. I was staring at the ceiling half unaware of my surroundings. "Don't be sad," he said, turning on his side. He rubbed my chest.

I turned to him with a slight smile. "I can't imagine what it will be like," I admitted, voice choking.

Cat pulled over closer to me and rested his head on my shoulder.

"I wish you could tell me everything would be okay and I would believe it," I whined.

"It *will* be okay," Cat asserted. "It won't be too long before you see me again. And when I get out of the navy and am focused we'll find a nice quiet place to live." He sighed. "But first we'll get married. It won't be one of those courthouse weddings, though. Our wedding will be huge. The wedding of the year. We'll have all of our favorite music. Hell, we'll get the artists to perform live! Emmylou *and* Mary Chapin Carpenter. For the main course we'll serve Mutt 'n' Slop."

He laughed, and I along with him.

What he was saying was nice. Very romantic. But I doubted he would ever have the fortitude to be wedded as openly and extravagantly as he said. Still, the thought had the effect he intended. It calmed me and made me smile.

"And then," I added to the fantasy, "a future of weeping willows and sipping sassafras tea on an old porch. Where will we live? Down south maybe?"

"Naw. Why don't we get a place on the east coast? A lighthouse. We could wear sweaters all day and eat stews and go to town meetings. We'll have enough land to own some horses and dogs. Big, energetic dogs that slobber and scare grown men. We'll name one Captain Badass," he chuckled, "and you can name one after that lover of Alexander the Great's. What was his name?"

"Hephaestion," I answered.

"Yeah...Hephaestion. Maybe we'll even have kids when we get older. There's plenty that need adopting, that need loving homes. And we'll travel, baby. We'll travel everywhere."

"And grow old together," I interjected, looking him in his beautiful eyes.

"And at the end, die in each other's arms." He kissed me at length.

"No," I said, "let's never die."

"Who says we ever do?" he whispered.

I let myself believe it for that moment. I sighed and looked back to the ceiling.

"Good," I whispered.

I stayed awake the entire night. Each minute raced into the next, colliding into one another. The night was all too quickly gone. I stared at Cat sleeping, wondering how he could possibly rest. I lay against his warm skin until the first light of day streamed through the window like an unwelcome guest.

I ran a finger along the scar on his shoulder. It was strange that the scar, that one flaw on his perfect flesh, made him all the more sexy and desirable to me. I leaned in closer and kissed it. Then I lifted the sheet we had slept beneath and took a last admiring glance at the tattoo on his thigh. I kissed it as well. Perhaps it was a sort of blessing. Perhaps I knew that it was the smaller things that I would miss most about him, the things he had always kept secret from the rest of the world.

In the bathroom, I splashed my face with water and looked into the mirror. This was for the best, I assured myself. In a few hours Cat would be taking a cab to the airport and then he would be gone. There would be no Hollywood kiss at the terminal. Our last kiss and last touch would need to be in private. A show of affection, of absolute devotion, not witnessed by the rest of the world.

He was frisky that morning. Ready and excited to start a new chapter in his life. We played around a little until the time had come to get serious and call the cab. In a few minutes it pulled up to the curb below. Cat and I kissed. I didn't want it to end.

We walked down to meet the waiting cab at the curb.

"Well," he said, his voice sounding strained, "here we are."

I began to well up. I was never a master of emotions such as he.

"Cat," was all I could get out before my throat closed on me.

He embraced me, a big, masculine hug.

"I'll write and call all the time. Every day," he promised.

I pulled from him just a little.

"I didn't want your last memory of me before you left to be a crying sissy," I said, smiling and wiping my eyes.

He looked at me sincerely.

"It won't be," he said.

What happened next was magic. He kissed me as hard as he had ever done. It was a great Hollywood good-bye. It was cinematic; it was Bogart and Bergman. It was all swelling music with not a dry eye in the house.

We separated and stared one last time at each other. He picked up his suitcase and placed it in the cab.

"Your ass is gonna look great in that uniform," I laughed through tears. I straightened up. "I love you, Cat," I said.

He smiled. Hell, he almost gleamed.

"I'll remember every part of you," he said, and added with a smile, "Keep that hat off the bed while I'm gone."

Then he ducked into the cab and waved as it drove away. I stood watching until I could no longer see the yellow car down the busy street.

Eric Arvin

A Jog in the Rain

I sighed, drifting out of my state of deep thought. The day had gone quiet and darkened. The sun was hidden by clouds. "A chance of rain," the weather woman on channel 32 had said. Just a chance. I heard a rumble of thunder call down to the earth. There hadn't been much rain this summer. Maybe it had all saved itself up for a deluge at the end. A great downpour that would flood the river and swallow the dry world. Each cloud refusing to dispense its containment until it was bursting. Perhaps now was the time. It *was* the end of the summer, after all. There had to be one good summer storm before the year was through.

And to me it was the end of the year as well. For some reason I had never grown out of the notion that summer's end was year's end. It was a holdover, I knew, from my years in school. I asked myself if it might also be a sign of never growing up. "You're so overdramatic!" I could hear Cat scream at me from miles away. And that was true. I was overdramatic. I always had a penchant for the theatrical when it came to my emotions. I was a stage show. Why else would I be in the old garage my father had built, staring at old boxes and belongings, remembering them, and holding a postcard I had received from Cat a week and a half earlier? A postcard that was already showing signs of being handled too much. *I was indeed dramatic!* Cat always teased me for this, and yet he accepted it. It made me wonder if he missed my big words and wide moods when, on the postcard, I saw he had written: ***Every part of you!***

They were his last words to me before he got in the cab weeks earlier. "I'll remember every part of you," he had said. He knew I would romanticize over those words for as long as he was gone.

I took the Verona baseball cap off my head. I had been wearing it a lot lately. I made a decision to grow my hair long until Cat returned. Though it had only been a few weeks since he had left, my hair had always grown fast, and it was now becoming unmanageable. I wore the hat to cover it and keep it down. There was no logical reason behind my decision not to cut my hair. It was something to do, I guess. A way of showing support. Or grief? For whatever reason, however, it was something, the only thing, I could control.

Everything was changing too quickly. Things were happening too fast. I couldn't keep up. That's what brought me to the point of my drama in the garage, I suppose. The barrage of life's unavoidable changes. I was set, within the week, to start my new job as a research assistant at a new school. I was panicked. Unsure, really, if I could do *anything* well. My life had been school and illness up to this point. How could I be sure I had what it took to make it out there alone? Things would somehow surely go wrong. There were so many things out of place.

If Cat were with me, by my side, he would encourage me, and soon everything would be fine. But he was not there, and I was alone and terrified. I could usually count on a call from Cat, at least weekly, to lift my spirits, but I had not heard from him since the postcard in my hand. My mind wandered everywhere looking for him. I had heard on the news of a blast, an accident, aboard a ship. *Could that have been Cat's ship? Was he done with training and now lying in a hospital near death?* I shivered. Such things had been the stuff of my nightmares since he had left. Now my uncertainty about other things in my own life were colliding and gelling with my fears of Cat's safety. Life now seemed like a well. Dry and barren and endless. A chasm of inexhaustible emptiness and discontentedness.

I heard a tiny drop hit the tin roof of the garage. Then another and another. Soon it was raining. Not a hard rain one would seek shelter from, but a soft, lovely rain. A soothing, cathartic rain. The kind one becomes part of. A comforting music was being played on the tin roof. Through all the worries and huge questions in my mind, a resolution of sorts presented itself: *a jog in the rain.*

Without hesitation, I left the garage behind and got into my car. I knew where it was I wanted to be. I knew exactly where I wanted to jog. The rain began to fall harder now. The wipers tried desperately to keep in sync with the CD I had grabbed on my way out of the garage. The CD for a rainy afternoon Cat had mixed for me years earlier.

The distance from my mother's house to the campus of my alma mater lapsed almost instantaneously. No sooner had I left the gravel lane of my childhood home than I arrived at the college. I pulled up to the shoulder of the road at the Point. For a moment I stared from my seat out at the river, winding its way through the valley and then disappearing into haze and a rainy mist. It was a muddy, majestic body, that river. Each drop of rain added to its great flow.

I got out of the car, still entranced by the sight of the river, flung off my shirt, and began to jog. My right leg was still weak. I could feel a slight limp, though it went unnoticed by the very few people on campus that saw me. School had yet to begin, and, for the most part, the campus was empty. The rain felt immediately soothing on my bare chest, shoulders, and back. I felt at the same time reinvigorated. As I jogged, the rain tapped and splashed various songs and melodies on the road and pavement. The raindrops whispered my own thoughts to me in a cadence.

Stress and density... stress and density... every part of you... great works of gods and men... stress and density....

I imagined Cat running along side of me, calming me. Telling me not to let it in, the stress. *Don't let it overtake. Be thick. Sometimes you're ahead, and sometimes not, and occasionally you lose sight of things, but everything eventually turns out for the best.* It was cliché, all of it, and Cat had never once said any of it, but still I imagined.

The rain continued to work its magic on my mind. The water streamed down my body and off the tips of my nose and eyelashes. Soon my hair was completely wet, and I ran my hand through it to push back some of the rain it had collected. It felt like a baptism. In a matter of moments while under the rain, I found my mood was beginning to change. I thought it amusing that I was so worried and sentimental earlier in the garage. Worrying about where I was 'supposed' to be in life seemed pointless now. Cat would say that I had battle scars that I should be proud of. And if Cat's burgeoning scientific theology was right, if everything was just matter and energy, then, in the end, there was plenty of time. Everything goes on and on forever, and time doesn't matter. This made my heart jump, and I smiled.

I realized I had done a poor job in accepting things. I distanced myself from trying times. Maybe, I thought, I should let all those things in. I should deal with them. Even though some memories it would seem easier and less painful to simply forget, I reminded myself, there is growth in those times, and powerful realizations as well. I felt a warmth moving up my spine.

"I am in no hurry to forget," I whispered to the rain.

It came to me that my plan had to go. Once and for all I needed to rid my mind of the last bastion of that outline I had written years earlier. Every last printed word had to be erased. It was a trap to the past. A snare of expectations. The important thing now, I thought, was to rid myself of the life that was planned so that I might at last have the life that was waiting. A life, I was sure, that would bring unexpected triumphs rather than foreseen fortunes. I could *want*. Wanting was fine, but the idea that I needed a certain future had to be released. I could want that house in Maine and everything Cat had lulled me into security with on our last night together, but it was wrong to expect it. It would put too much weight on me, on Cat, on us. It would be an immoral thing for me to demand any future other than what was to be of its own fruition. I staked a sign post in my mind to never again expect anything.

My whole body felt refreshed. I felt that cleansed feeling again, like deep breathing after a hard cry. Only, I hadn't shed a tear. I was overcome with a sensation of power. My will, my strength had pulled me out of greater problems than this. Twice I had risen from personal devastation. Leaving my life as I had known it would be scary, but I had strength. I thought back to when I was recovering from my illness. Cat was with me at a physical therapy visit. There was an old man, Mr. Grace, who had suffered too many strokes. And I remembered Cat looking at me slyly. If that old man could pull through then...*I could do this!* And I could and would have to do it alone.

I had jogged back to the car, a full circle around the small campus. The river would be in sight. Already I could glimpse it through the brush and trees that grew up on the hill from the valley. I was emerging from a thick fog I had been in most of my life. A fog as thick as that over the river and the hills and valley on early summer mornings. It was a wonderful moment. It was at that moment that I knew; I was certain that the Great Mystery, God, reveals itself not in fantastic happenings and miracles, but in slight details and random events. That's life, after all. Life is the small things, not the things *I* had been concerned with. Life was Emmylou Harris on a mixed CD; it was contained in annoying habits; in poems; in an idea; a great recipe; a high after a workout; a scar on a shoulder; the colors in a butterfly tattoo; it was in sunsets and sunrises; the smell of fried onions; and life was certainly all about a jog in the rain. The large events of life are but the bookmarks between chapters.

My car was just ahead. I stopped jogging and walked the rest of the way to the Point. *Where to now?* It was not a melancholy question but one that filled me with excitement. I remembered Cat saying something to me once as we sat on the grass watching the river. It was during that great summer after one of our jogs. He looked over to me and smiled. "I'm like a river, you know," he said mischievously.

"How's that?" I responded.

"I wind up all over the place." He laughed. I shook my head in playful disapproval. I was sure he had heard it from somewhere and stolen credit for it. The statement stuck with me, though, and seemed very relevant.

I sat down on the wet ground, and began to cry like a big, happy baby. I raised my face to the sky, closed my eyes, and let the rain wash my tears away. There was a light vibration in my pocket. It took me a moment to remember I had my cell phone on me. I was tempted to ignore it and continue my worship of the rain and my new philosophy. But I gave in and answered.

"Hey Baby," Cat said gently from the other end. I was overjoyed. It was a perfect moment. A gentle rumble of thunder passed through the clouds above me.

"Hey," I sputtered out, not even trying to disguise my emotion.

"Why are you crying?"

"I'm...it's great to hear your voice," I laughed.

"Yeah. You too. Sorry I wasn't able to call sooner. I can only imagine what you've been thinking," he teased. He knew quite well what I had been thinking.

"And you'd be right. So tell me everything. Everything that's happened. Every minute...." I was relieved, and my voice made that apparent. As we talked, it all felt right and perfect and in place. The unexpectedness of the moment was fantastic. Everything was accessible now. It was all do-able, and I was growing certain, too, that I was going to be able to do it. This new future, this new look of my life, was livable. With every word he spoke I was stronger. There it was, at last! I was happy. Exceedingly so. Yes, *at last,* happy, wet, in love and without a plan...

...and there's no telling where the day might end.

indecision

I decided
I must have
To pry my way out
On the sixth day
The sixth of may
Nine months in the juices
Was quite enough
God let me tumble
Round rosy bundle
Into tougher stuff

On the sixth of may
Hindenburg, 1937:
Let that be my lesson

What juice can I squeeze
Thus far from life
On a high branch
I can't see for the sun
The moment-by-moment
disasters
That await me

I could accomplish
And conquer oblivion or
Hang around until
All the juice is sour

All this juice
Wrapped in tight
And I'm still too green
Too scared of the forbidden

In the sky
Staring god in the eye
How will it hurt
My trip to the earth
Will I black out from it all
The excitement of the fall
Or am I in danger of not falling
at all.

Eric Arvin

Late Bloomer in the Water

HE learned to swim at the clever age of twenty-eight. Gail Harm was always a late bloomer. He was kept from the water by fear and doubt, by an anxiety he could never quite name. A false sense of insecurity. He observed others, how they found their pace in the current, how they managed, and he respected them for it. Indeed, he felt something resembling awe toward them. But he never ventured into the water himself. Best to let those who know the water do the swimming.

When he was younger – when all the other boys were learning to tread water at the pool – he stood at the side, shuddering more from embarrassment of being topless, exposed, than from any actual coolness of air on skin. His parents and friends had tried to encourage him. At so young an age, though, encouragement and threats are hard to differentiate through a veil of fear. No one ever got him to take so much as a toe-dip in the pool. Not once. He would watch the other swimmers with envy; he would watch televised swimming events with a sense of shame. Why could he not do it? Why could he never dive in? His adult life had continued to be just like that. Poolside shivers and self-conscious eyes. Stressing over the details and flaws, the exposure, that no one else seemed to notice. Or if they did, they never cared.

But then, at the age of twenty-eight – yes, that late – Gail blossomed forth.

He shot up through the internalized phobias that others had unknowingly planted in him and went swimming in a small pond. Dove in for the very first time. The fact that he knew how to swim was not a surprise. He had watched other boys, now men, in the water all his life. He knew a breaststroke from a backstroke. What did surprise him was how perfect it felt. The moment he hit the water, that glorious splash scattered his inhibitions. Naked, and okay with being naked. Perfectly fine with being a twenty-eight year old, naked, late bloomer in the water.

On the opposite bank, watching him, lovingly encouraging him without a hint of threat, was the springboard to Gail's awakening. Marsh Gary.

To Gail's astonishment, Marsh had begun undressing right there on the banks of the pond as they walked around it on that late afternoon. The summer was kind. It hadn't been too hot, and a breeze caused ripples on the water. Marsh took every piece of clothing off slowly, as if it were nothing, as if he were in his room readying for bed. He kept his eyes locked to Gail's, and he smiled.

"What are you doing?" Gail asked breathlessly. Forbidden things surfaced in his mind. As forbidden to himself as the touch of water.

"I'm going swimming," Marsh teased. "Meet me on the other side?" Gail wondered if that was a question intent on making him jump in as well. He could just as easily walk around the pond and meet Marsh there.

Marsh ran and jumped into the pond, his body elongated and elegant. Gail was burning up just looking at him. He watched Marsh cross the water with ease. Such beauty and grace. When he climbed onto the opposite bank he waved Gail over, his skin shining. Forbidden, but how sweet the touch must be.

"I don't know how," Gail shouted across the pond. "I don't know how to swim."

"You never learned?" Had he never told Marsh? But then, why would he have?

"Never." But something in Gail told him he knew how to do it.

"It's nothing. You can do it. It's the most natural thing in the world, Gail. We're all born in liquid, after all. It's like swimming through oxygen, just heavier."

"But what if I sink?"

Frogs and birds listened with anticipation.

"I'm here," Marsh assured him. "I'm right here, and I'll help you."

Gail didn't understand why Marsh's assurance was all he needed to hear. It made no sense that that alone would ease his fear, his trepidation. But it did. He no longer felt the dread; it dripped away.

Gail quickly disrobed. His was not the easy, graceful disrobing that Marsh had performed. No, his was frenzied and clumsy. But once he was totally nude he stood erect, proud, as if showing off to Marsh. As if saying "Look what I can do!" A phrase he had never proclaimed as a child.

"Come on then! Jump in! I'm right here. Just come to me."

And so Gail dove in. Marsh was right. The water felt true. It felt natural. Why had he refused it for so long? Sure, it was muddy and murky, but that no longer seemed to bother him. He could get through it the same as everyone else.

He swam, and he was good at it. Marsh watched him, smiling, returning the grin that Gail wore even as his face was submerged beneath the pond water. He was doing it; he was swimming. But that realization and its companion thought that he had missed so much by avoiding the water all these years made him fumble. He jerked with fear and seemed to forget what it was he was doing.

He began to struggle; he began to panic.

"Calm down!" Marsh shouted from the shore. "You're doing fine. You're doing great."

But Gail could not regain his composure and security. He began to sink. And he thought the water was there to tease him all along, just to get him to dive in so he would drown.

As he struggled, he heard a splash and soon felt the comforting strength of an arm around his neck, pulling him to the pond bank. Marsh looked down upon Gail as he lay on the ground, breathing, rasping. The realization that he had survived excited him.

"You're okay," Marsh said. "See? You're okay. You did it."

Gail said nothing. He stared into Marsh's face, into the kindness, the understanding. He cherished each drop of water that fell from Marsh's nose and eyelashes onto his own flesh. Without embarrassment, he enjoyed the feel of Marsh's wet, naked form on top of his own, of Marsh's hand stroking his hair.

Of Marsh's lips on his. Wet lips, kissing gently but strong.

"Now," Marsh whispered, not more than an inch from Gail's face, "aren't you glad you jumped in?"

Eric Arvin

Butterfly Tattoo

There were so many things about him that made me sigh, but nothing more so than the butterfly tattoo on his thigh.

There were so many pieces to him. Like a beautiful puzzle.

His eyes – those that caught me like visionary cast line – while I waited in line in the dining hall. Blue and sharp as icicles, but gentle as tears. (I kissed those lids once on a stormy evening when the electricity had gone out.)

His lips were full, especially the bottom one. Oh, to suck and tug on that once more! He was in a brawl once in some seedy bar. I tended his lip carefully. It was tender for a while after.

I ruffled my hands through his thick black hair. He would let it grow sometimes; shoulder-length. He always used an apple-scented shampoo. He had wanted to pepper it with highlights, but I managed to talk him out of it.

I layered kisses and nibbles on his jaw and neck. He would simply melt whenever I sucked on his throat. But my favorite spot was just behind the ear. A sweet, come-from-behind and then a sneak attack on those precious lobes.

His shoulders were always strong and broad. Years of ball playing had sculpted them. When summer came he was a bronzed god. Apollo, or maybe Atlas.

His arms – biceps and triceps and forearms – were tough and vascular. I would lick on the muscled peaks and play with the veins, tracing them to the sensitive underside of his arms.

His hands were large; like a bushel of salty lollipops.

I would kiss his underarms. Nuzzle up to them at night, smelling the scent of him. God, how I miss that scent!

His back was a wall of muscle. It rippled with striations if he barely moved. I would draw my finger down the spine to give him chills, and then trace the trail with kisses.

His chest I would sleep on occasionally. And when he ran the pectorals bounced and moved. I could hardly keep myself calm. The nipples were large and pleaded to be sucked and flicked. The great valley between his pecs was deep. (Once he had brought me a bouquet of flowers positioned there between the meat. It made me laugh.)

His abdomen was hard as stone. He got in a gut-punching match once with another player just to see how much they could endure.

The fine hairs from his belly button led down to a splendid package. It was more than I could handle, but I never failed to try and use every inch of it. (I succeeded in getting it all in once. We celebrated with a fast furious fuck, and I couldn't walk right for a week.) When he was inside of me – or I in him – it was the closest to God I ever knew.

His ass was round and full. It jiggled when I came into him. My fingers pierced the flesh; I loved the fullness of it. His pants – khakis or sweats or blue jeans – always needed to accommodate his backside, so he needed a size larger than his 32-inch waist.

His legs were steel and could squeeze the life out of anything. I felt secure between them, though. I shaved them a few times, just so I could more clearly see the muscle beneath the hair.

Eric Arvin

But it was his inner thigh that attracted me most. The butterfly. Such delicacy painted into such strength. I could gain control of him through it as if it were a switch or a button. When I would kiss and lick the butterfly tattoo, he would absolutely rock in ecstasy. It was only a small thing colored a deep purple, but oh, the joyful fury that button could unleash. (I once made him gush just by sucking on it.)

He would moan and moan. And I would kiss and suck and lick and whisper onto it, "I love you... I love you... I love you."

Books by Covers

JIMMY stretched his leg muscles on the steps in front of his apartment, releasing the tension for the torture. A good run on this spring afternoon would be just what he needed. It was a beautiful day, offering lovely promises. He could run for a while and clear the obstacles, the hurdles, in his mind. He often wondered when it was the real world started taking control of his psyche, regulating his inner thoughts until they mirrored one another. Had it happened innocently? Little by little? Or was it, as he had always suspected, clump by clump?

Runners don't like clumps. They're unexpected. Clumps can make a runner trip and fall.

Forget the world, he told himself. Forget the world you see. Forget the world as it's reflected in your mind. Clarity. That's what you need.

Jimmy set off tracking that clarity. He didn't think he'd truly find it. The answers to his questions and concerns seemed too big. He'd been troubled for weeks after all. Still, a jog could help him think, to ponder. Jimmy needed that alone time. The small college town went on around him – mothers and children on sidewalks, the postman delivering his packages, cars driving leisurely past, college students off campus interacting with the townsfolk. So serene and just so. Like a film set or TV show from the fifties.

Jimmy headed in the direction of the liberal arts school. He had chosen to go to a larger university. Got his B.A. at a prestigious school up north, but dropped out of grad school before he could get his master's. He regretted that. But at the time he just couldn't do it anymore. He had had enough of education. He had been sidetracked by other things. Like the full-time gig at the fashionable clothing store to help pay off his increasing credit card debt. Or the insurance for the sports car he no longer thought of as his baby. Now, though, he desperately needed to get back to school. He envied teachers and college professors who were surrounded by academia at all times. He was in need of a real job, a career. Especially with the wedding coming up. Gunner had his heart set on a house, an expensive house. A house so expensive both of them would have to sell their souls to obtain it. But for Gunner, Jimmy would do it. Jimmy did a lot of things for Gunner.

Sidetracked. Short cuts.

PROFESSOR ROBBINS taught classic literature at the college. She was normally a content person. She had a nice, quiet life with a loving partner who she had met at Pride years ago; she had a smart, young daughter; she had a nice home on the college campus; and she adored her students. She loved the looks on their faces when they learned something new. That spark of epiphany that doesn't happen but every so often; just enough to make it precious and longed for. Yes, she was usually happy with her life's course. She had designed it.

But as she stared out the window over the heads of the small classroom of students taking an exam, she saw a handsome young man jog by. It wasn't the man that stalled her, really. Her tastes didn't run his way. It was his seeming physical perfection, his lack of flaws that captivated her. He looked like a sculpture, the kind she had struggled to create in her undergraduate career. She had so wanted to be a great artist. She studied the classics – Rodin, Michelangelo, Bernini – but she could never quite get it right. All her life it had been her dream to bring life from stone; her hands working an almost divine thing. Like a goddess.

But life in its pushy way convinced her to try other things. It prodded her in a more logical direction. Something which might bring more money and stability. Successful artists are rare, she heard over and over. Art is ever changing because tastes and fads change daily, hourly. An artist would be unemployable, she was told. Especially a sculptor. Who sculpts nowadays? There are machines for that.

He does, Professor Robbins said to herself defensively. This young man jogging. He sculpts his body every day in the gym. Like art, it takes skill, study, persistence, and time. He must be so joyous. The world gets to see his sculpture everywhere he goes. A great artist runs among us today. Don't you see?

But no one would ever see. No one saw the world and its unfairness as well as she.

She closed her eyes. Dreams leave me alone. I'm happy. I'm quite content.

THE college lawn was always Jimmy's favorite part of the campus. Everyone was carefree as they studied or lounged on the grass. Their minds caught up in frivolous pursuits. Not a notion that things might get worse in the future. He remembered the future in college sounded to him like an obscure idea; something other people thought about. Something that was whispered with hushed dread, but never truly confronted.

Plan for the future? An impossibility. How can one plan for what they don't know or have never experienced?

Jimmy felt envious of the students on the lawn, of the boys tossing Frisbees over the heads of lovers. He wanted to sit among them again, to feel that blissful unawareness. But he also worried for them. How many would survive after college? How many could surmount the world's bulky hurdles?

Dotting the lawn like wildflowers, the coupled lovers kissing made him think of his relationship with Gunner. Would they stay as passionate? He wanted a lifelong romance. (Oh, how Hollywood has ruined that word!) Would it happen? Would Gunner stay with him till the end? Would Jimmy want him to?

ELISE watched the man jogging. She wasn't the only one, but she was most likely the only one not lusting, not hooting and making vulgar noises. A gaggle of girls on the south side of the lawn were doing enough of that. Elise was instead struck by the runner's resemblance to her high school sweetheart. A twinge of bittersweet remorse enfolded her heart. The chemistry book on her lap suddenly felt heavier, less about her future and more about things left behind.

She was a senior now. She hadn't seen Bud for over three years. She left him the summer before her freshman year saying she had to go. She had to get out of the small town she had grown up in. There was nothing for her there. Those were painful words to say. She realized they were probably even more painful to hear.

"There's me. I'm here," Bud had pleaded.

That wasn't enough. She didn't understand why he didn't understand. She had loved him. And now this runner was breaking her heart, and he didn't even know it.

Elise couldn't imagine ever feeling the way she felt about Bud toward anyone else. The world was filled with little boys and tiny men. Bud was different, mature. He was as wonderful as any woman could have hoped. He wanted to marry her. She had wanted the same once.

What happened?

She knew she shouldn't regret her choices. College was always down the road for her in high school. But still, the runner was making it hard to forget lost chances. She tried to look away. She tried to focus on the body, not the face. Bud and the runner didn't have the same body. Bud was strong from years of farm work, not weights.

Elise imagined the runner had never made a bad choice in his life. Mr. Perfect with his perfect body, his perfectly planned life.

That's what she chose to believe.

THE wedding was only two months away. Still too soon for Jimmy. Not that he didn't want to pledge himself to Gunner. No, he wanted it more than anything, but there was just so much to do. There was a life neither of them could see that needed to be planned out.

"We'll get by," Gunner always said.

Money doesn't fall from trees. You have to climb up to get it.

All their arguments lately had turned into fights. Fights about money. It could get bad. Fists could fly over money, over what needed to be done with it or how much should be spent when. Whenever Jimmy brought Gunner a gift, Gunner reminded him the money spent could have been used toward the house.

Gunner's big, beautiful house that he had to have.

Jimmy tried to shirk the thought of that house off, to leave it behind on the college lawn as he ran. But it kept up the pace. Worries seem to be able to do that. They're more up to a challenge than clarity. Clarity is free and unbothered. It drifts; it doesn't run.

The way Jimmy saw it, they couldn't both afford to go back to school. Gunner had already started with his new degree. But to afford that house, they both would have to get much better jobs. And Jimmy couldn't get a better job without going back to school.

Circles and circles, running in circles.

Jimmy really didn't want the house. It was very nice. He agreed with Gunner about that. But a nice apartment would have been better. In the long run, a new, larger apartment would be better both financially and for their relationship. Funny how money can take dreams and love apart like dissection.

Love is all finances now.

Jimmy ran past the new construction site on campus. A state-of-the-art science building was going up, replacing the old one. He didn't understand why. The old one was nice. The construction workers were on a break. They whistled and catcalled at Jimmy.

"Nice tits!" one yelled. The others cackled in macho solidarity. There was contempt beneath those laughs.

BULL. That's what they called him because that's what he looked like. A big angry bull.

"Nice tits," his fellow construction workers repeated what he said in a congratulatory manner. As if it were the most brilliant thing ever muttered, and they wanted to remember it. They'd repeat the story at the bar that night.

Bull smiled, accepted their compliments, but he didn't feel like a clever man. He felt full of doubts upon seeing the young man jog past. He wasn't always a bull. He was healthy and young once, too. He had a body others admired at one time, just like the runner. Girls loved him. But now, after years of neglect and bad habits, that body had disappeared beneath layers of another. Where had he gone? Not this flabby man sitting on scaffolding in the sun, but the man he was, the man he truly was, who had a sense of pride in how he looked. Where had *that* man gone?

This happened, he thought, as he took a huge bite of his double bacon cheeseburger. Life. Family. Responsibility. Everything that young runner was yet to find, if he ever would. He looked the type to never have problems.

Bull had looked like that once. Had people thought the same of him? That he never had problems? In Bull's life, things were not handed to him. Things were earned or taken. Lots of things were taken. His little girl after his wife left him; all the money his ex-wife took from him each month; dignity; looks; health.

The doctor told him he'd have a heart attack if he didn't start eating right. He was too overweight, his cholesterol too high.

Bull looked at his burger. He remembered a time when he was concerned with his health. He should try to be concerned again. But it was hard now. He would never get his body back anyway; he would never find his former self hiding within.

Why try?

NICE tits. Funny. Jimmy smiled, trekking onward toward the baseball diamond. He had to admit his pectorals, though all muscle, did bounce when he ran. Tits are tits to straight men. He could have been offended, but why bother. Those construction workers probably had so little fun in their lives, so little real purpose, that he would allow them their fun at his expense. At least the remark had momentarily distracted him from his problems.

He respected construction workers. Theirs was a hard job. A job with an estimable outcome. Something that might benefit society. Jimmy couldn't say the same about his own job, his non-career. Managing a clothing store. What was so special about that? Day after day of hearing Little Susie Gotta-have-its gush over designer clothes. All his years of education, of being told by countless teachers that he could change the world, and what? Teachers lie. It's their job.

The world changes without you just fine. You're a colonist. A useless colonist. You're a faceless runner in the Boston marathon.

The college baseball team was at practice. Hot young guys in shorts that molded their asses deliciously. But Jimmy wasn't in the mood to gawk. Even if he was, he wasn't too attracted to the younger set anymore. Besides, ball players had only space enough in their brains for a few things. Baseball, women, and doping.

Stereotypes play out before us. We accept them because we choose to.

Jimmy wished his mind was that vacant. He wished he could forget everything. Everything but men. Then he'd be a stereotype, too. Just what the world wanted. He wished he could forget Gunner for a moment. He wished Gunner's house away. Fallen down. Burnt down. Torpedoed.

Play ball, boys. Enjoy it.

TREVOR watched the muscle man jog past. He was readying to practice his swing, but the pitcher wasn't ready. Trevor had seen the runner before. He must be from town, he thought. A townie. Townies like being around the college boys.

Trevor didn't understand why he couldn't look away. But when the muscle man came into view he had to watch. He was mesmerized by the mass of the man. He felt an uncomfortable tightness in his shorts. Thank God for his jock strap or the guys would think he was getting a boner staring at the muscle man. They couldn't see it, but he felt it. Usually that excitement was a good thing, but he felt bothered by it in this instance.

Eric Arvin

I'm not gay. I'm not gay. But I bet he is.

Earlier in the day Trevor had taunted a classmate at lunch. One of the gay kids, out and open about it at the small college.

He was asking for it. It's just teasing. He'll survive.

Trevor was certain the kid was looking at him, leering. The kid wanted him. All the gay boys had a thing for him. He was sure about that. So this muscle jogger must have a thing for him, too.

Were there such a thing as gay vibes? Homo-radio waves? Maybe the runner was sending his waves to Trevor.

Why did he feel so bad after he mocked the gay kid? After he called him names in front of everyone. The kid deserved it, right? Like this runner. Flaunting himself in front of the college boys. Trying to get noticed.

Which way's the gym? Follow me to the locker room.

Trevor couldn't stop watching the runner's chest. How it bounced and moved. Beautiful. Could another man be beautiful?

Did I just think that? Why am I hard?

Trevor didn't hear the pitcher say he was ready, though he raised the bat at the sound of his voice. His attention was still on the runner's chest and his own crotch. But he definitely felt the pain as the ball nailed him in the testicles.

Oh, God! I'm gay.

JIMMY stopped near the woods that bordered the campus. He needed a rest from all the voices in his head. All the 'what-to-dos'. He took a deep breath and let in decision. It flowed through him like clarity. He knew what he had to do because there was simply no way around it. Appearances be damned.

They would make it past this bump in the road. He and Gunner would have a great life together, and their wedding would be gorgeous. As big as Gunner wanted. They'd splurge. They'd use the money they were going to use for the house.

The house they would not be getting.

Gunner could hate him for a few days. That was preferable to Gunner hating him for the rest of their lives simply because finances had driven a wedge between them. Jimmy would explain this. Somehow, Gunner would understand. Surely, he would. Gunner was short-sighted but he wasn't ignorant.

"And," Jimmy thought, "it's my life too. I'll make him happy without a house."

They could even go to school together. Both of them. Classmates.

But first he would have to think about when to break the news he had received that morning.

The doctor said, "Jimmy, you have a lump on your testicle."

God, when to tell Gunner! He'll fold. I know Gunner. Know him like a book.

Eric Arvin

The Ice Tree

FOR Perry, winter was the season for cutting wood with his father, a large, fleshy man with a strict but loving manner. It was a tedious chore made all the more so by the fact that the time was spent listening to religious lectures between the buzz of the saw. They lived back a long, graveled lane away from the main road. On both sides of the lane towered stoic, indifferent trees. All of Perry's early life, the old storybook house had been heated in the winter months by a wood stove. So, in the colder months he found himself fighting not only snow, but sawdust and God.

Though the resentment was strong, the falling out between Perry and his father was a gradual descent rather than a quick-rushing crash.

His father sat in the dark kitchen every night reading his Bible. He would always drink hot tea from the same mug like a prized grail. It wasn't anything special, really. Just a plain white china coffee mug. Written in blue dye on the rounded base was **McNicol China Clarksburg, W. Va. 56**. The mug was almost an extension of him. If he was at home, not working at the factory or cutting wood, it would have been very strange not to see him carrying the mug around, steam rising. Perry thought on more than one occasion that they resembled one another; heavy and comfortable in weight; thick and stout.

It had been an almost unbearable cold season. The freeze in the air made it impossible to stay outside for any length of time. The snow fell thick and heavy. Ice brought the trees down to the ground. The weather was as resentful as the world it fell upon. Even the wind that made its ricochet-way through the hills of the river valley assailed the small house with an angry howl.

Perry listened to the howling outside as he sat in the kitchen, eating a snack of buttered toast and tomatoes before going to bed. He was content in his solitude. A small night light was the only light in the room; he rather liked the feeling of being hidden and alone. But his father's loud, approaching footsteps broke the silence. As he came into the kitchen, the old wood floors could hardly support his heavy frame. He coughed roughly. Perry's mother thought he might have caught the flu.

He coughed again, this time a little louder. Then he saw his son at the table. "Hey there!" he said cheerfully. He poured some hot tea from the pot on the stove into his mug.

Perry mumbled something almost inaudible, but it was enough for his father. At least Perry wasn't ignoring him. He still had the broad, welcoming smile that delighted Perry as a child, but now Perry found himself resenting it. That smile was a trap; it led to lectures and conversations about God. So Perry learned to not respond to it.

It never occurred to Perry how alone his father must have felt that cold winter evening.

"Do you want to go get some kindling with me this weekend? Mr. Haplin has some we could use all ready. We don't even need to saw it up."

"Dad, you're sick. And I have to work this weekend anyway." That was a lie. What he really meant was, *I hate being around you*.

"Well, we can go early in the morning." He coughed.

"Dad, it's too cold. And I want to sleep in this weekend."

His father breathed heavily. He was still smiling, but now looking directly at Perry instead of dividing his attention between his mug and his son. "I need help. Your brother's not going to be able to come over with the roads the way they are. All we need to do is get in the truck and get the wood. It's just right down the road."

"Whatever," Perry said, getting up and leaving the rest of his snack uneaten on the table.

The following evening, a Friday, Perry's father called in sick. Again, Perry was in the kitchen having a late night snack. Everyone else save his father was in the living room watching television. Perry moaned, thinking he would be getting up early the next day to get the wood from the Haplins.

As Perry took a bite from his toast, he heard a strange sound coming from his parents' bedroom. A groan, then a gasp, and then a noise and shake as if a great weight had fallen to the floor. No one else seemed to hear it. Perry slowly got up; cautious, as if I were about to get caught stealing a cookie from the old green glass jar on the counter.

Perry entered the dark room, and his eyes focused on outlines of images. In the suddenness of the moment, he could not immediately grasp what he was seeing. But soon it dawned on him. There on the floor, with his back against the side of the bed, was his father in a white T-shirt and underwear. His head was bowed as if his neck could not support it. His arms and legs were limp. One leg was straight out from him, the other folded under. Both arms rested with palms up. It was as if he had tried to get up from the bed, but instead collapsed off the edge of the mattress. He was mumbling something incoherent.

"Dad?" Perry whispered. There was no response except the moaning. "Mom! Mom! Something's wrong with Dad!"

There was a slight pause in existence; like time was collecting its breath. Then the panic of rushing feet could be heard. His mother hurried to the room, his sister in tow. They saw the large, collapsed form. The air in the room grew thin. His mother turned on the lamp, but it brought no clarity. It only added to the vertigo.

"Help me get him on the bed, hon," his mother uttered.

Perry took one arm and his mother took the other. With all their might they tried to get him back on the bed. Breathless and beginning to panic, Perry's mother massaged her forehead in thought.

"You stay here with him. I'll get help." She rushed off to the kitchen phone. Perry's sister Becca stood in the doorway, not knowing what to do. Their father was still mumbling. He was aware, yet helpless.

Perry's mother was on the phone with an ambulance dispatcher. Quickly, she hung up the phone and rushed back to the bedroom.

"Let's try and get him on the bed again," she said, even more out of breath.

With all of their strength they lifted him again. Becca helped. This time, somehow, they succeeded. As soon as he was on the bed, they heard sobbing. *He was sobbing.* His wife's heart folded there. She sat down beside him on the bed. "Bathroom... bathroom..." her husband sputtered out. He had been trying to get to the bathroom when he had collapsed to the floor.

"I know, honey. I'm sorry," she whispered. But there was no way to get him to the bathroom. "Shhhh," she breathed out against choked tears. She leaned over and kissed him gently on the mouth, then sat there beside him and ran her fingers through his peppered hair as he continued to quietly sob.

Perry sat down on the other side of his father. Becca sat on the floor by the bed. The snow fell outside, and a different kind of chill crept into the house. The dog began to moan from the wood shed.

PERRY stayed with his family that night at the hospital, waiting for any more word on the improvement of his father's condition after having slipped into a coma. The next day, he decided to get a ride with his older brother Lucas back home. He was going to check up on things at the house, feed the dog, and get everyone a change of clothes.

It was getting dark again as Lucas and Perry headed back to the house. The snow storm was over, and the plows and salt-trucks had been out doing what it was they did. The headlights of the passing vehicles streaked passed corners of wispy eyes like time running backward.

CHRISTMAS DAY came without any notice other than casual acceptance.

The day after Christmas, a quiet, unsplendid Sunday morning, Perry was again back home. He had been to the hospital several times, but still, he couldn't bring himself to visit his comatose father who had been asleep for a week. Lucas and Perry were readying themselves to head once again to the hospital.

Perry sat by a window in the living room, watching the icicles melt off the limbs of the giant maple tree in the front yard. As children, he and his siblings had climbed and played on it, and it grew along with them. Now it was in its prime and proud. In the spring it was flushed with green, in the fall it was brightly displayed, and in the winter, it took on a chilly coat of white. Every so often, an entire branch would shed the ice that clung to it. It was so easy for the ice to slip away even though, for a matter of days, it had grasped so unyielding to the branch. But now the separation was so effortless.

What a thing it must be to no longer need so desperately, Perry thought.

The phone broke Perry's trance out the window. Lucas ran to answer the call. But Perry already knew that good news seldom comes on quiet Sunday mornings or when the moon is high in the sky.

He heard the sound of Lucas' footsteps and turned to see him in the doorway. Lucas stared at the floor. "Dad died this morning...early."

Perry kept his gaze on the doorway long after Lucas had left it. It had actually happened. His father was gone, and it was real. Or at least it was possible. But was it realistic? How could he believe it? How could he ever be asked to understand it?

He felt like ice clinging to a branch, and he couldn't let go. How odd that he couldn't let go.

Raspberry Boy

"BRYCE, I gotta piss," Nate said. "I mean, I gotta go real bad."

He'd been trying to hold it as long as he could. Getting up in his condition from a hospital bed was not an easy task, and he absolutely refused to use a bed pan. Bryce and Nate had argued about his stubbornness on this matter, but in the end Nate had won. Nate always won. He was a Taurus. His stubborn streak left burn marks.

Bryce looked away from the mounted television where flickered some innocuous brain melt that passed these days for entertainment. "What do you want me to do?" he asked. "Do you want the nurse?" He shifted in the chair, preparing to rise.

"No." Nate glared. Hidden somewhere in that irritated glare was a heartbreaking plea. A plea that said, *Just you. I just need you.*

Bryce rose from his seat. It wasn't very comfortable anyway. Nate put his feet to the floor gently. When he was well he would have swung his feet around and hopped up immediately. But there was no swinging now, and certainly no hopping. Nate was in the hospital battling pneumonia. He had been too obstinate when he first began feeling bad to go to the doctor, so it had continued to worsen until finally Bryce had insisted on driving him to the hospital. Nate's blood oxygen level was dangerously low.

When he was admitted at once into intensive care, Bryce called him a dumbass. It wasn't an insult. That word had never been spoken before with such love and concern.

The pneumonia wasn't the cause of Nate's debilitation, though. No, he had been sick for a while before that. Pneumonia was simply an added thorn in the briar patch. Before a year ago Nate was always the picture of health, never missing a workout, until he had been sidelined by a malformation of blood vessels that had wrapped themselves around his medulla oblongata. A cluster, the doctor said. Looks like a raspberry.

"Ain't that some bullshit?" Nate said there in the doctor's office, staring at Bryce with stern but tired eyes that hid fear. Bryce could see the fear. Bryce was scared, too.

Now every step was a struggle for Nate. Vertigo and imbalance were ever present. It was a two-man balancing act.

"If I fall will you catch me?"

"I'll be waiting."

"Time after time?"

The need to use the bathroom made Nate try and walk faster than he knew he was able. The pressure on his bladder combined with the effects of the pneumonia and the vertigo issues made for an anxious stroll.

"Slow down. You'll hurt yourself."

"Shut up. I'm gonna piss myself. Why does the pisser gotta be so far away from the bed?"

"We're almost there, baby." Please get better, please get better, Bryce thought. With every step he thought it. Every morning when he woke up he thought it.

"I see it," Nate growled. You love me, I know you love me, he thought. And we're too young for life to be this serious.

He often wondered why Bryce stayed with him. He knew he was a gripe, a hassle to deal with. Why wasn't Bryce out doing other things? Doing other guys?

You love me.

I love you. Of course, I love you.

At the bathroom door Bryce waited. He made certain Nate was safely inside. "Sit down," he said. He still held to Nate's gown.

"I'm not sitting down!" Nate shot back. "I'll piss like a man."

Bryce shook his head and sighed. The door clicked shut. Bryce waited anxiously outside.

Nate knew Bryce was listening at the door, hoping against hope that he wouldn't fall. Listening for a thick steady stream to hit the toilet water. Nate wanted to cry in this rare moment of privacy. No, not cry. Weep. He wanted to weep. He wanted to weep for everything he wasn't anymore and for everything he couldn't be for Bryce. He didn't want this life for Bryce. He didn't want him worrying about him so.

Just leave me. It's okay if you leave me. Then I'll die, and it will be over.

He steadied himself with a hand on the sink. Thankfully it was close to the toilet. With his other hand he raised the gown and readied himself for the joyous, rapturous release that was to come. But just as he sighed in relief he lost his balance. In his attempt to stay on his feet and avoid falling backward, Nate let go of the sink, and his arms flailed in the air. His bladder, now unwilling to hold his water any longer, let loose the stream. In that moment Nate looked like a tumbling windmill on top of a fountain. Arms and liquid flying in every direction. He didn't know what to try and salvage first, his stance or control over his momentarily crazed penis. When he had at last stayed himself he had at least emptied his bladder...all over his nightgown.

Nate looked down at his soaking gown, then at his image in the mirror over the sink. Slowly, carefully he lowered himself onto the toilet seat. He stared vacantly ahead for a moment and then began to laugh. It was a curious sensation. He couldn't remember laughing for over a year. And this wasn't just chuckling. This was a full-out guttural belly-laugh.

Bryce, startled by the strange sound coming from the bathroom, pounded on the door. "Nate! Nate! Are you okay?"

"Yeah," Nate choked out between laughs. "I just need a new gown."

"Why? What happened? Are you sure you're okay?" Bryce feared Nate might have had a seizure; something the experts had said was a possibility.

Nate could hear the near panic in his partner's voice. He opened the door so Bryce could look in, and smiled up at him from the toilet. "I'm fine, baby," he said gently. "I'm just fine."

And he was. He really was.

Eric Arvin

Growl

Last night I dreamed you lingered back to me
And the dream had the shades of dawn
Beginning blue and hazy grey light
And we were hazy, crazy baby
Your lazy head on my chest and butterfly
Tattoo on your muscled thigh
Making dead poets green

Honeysuckle Sycamore

I

IN certain places of the world Passions manifest themselves into physical form. These are the whispering places, the in-betweens. They are neither here nor there, neither truly seen nor unseen. The River Valley, as it was simply known, was one of these places. The folk who lived there knew of the valley's power and, for the most part, lived in harmony with it. For the Passions when given form were in the least playful diversions and at most mischievous jokers, using a pumpkin patch for a night's sleep or stealing the clothes from a scarecrow.

Once every so often, however, there came a Passion into existence that was so dire, so hateful and belligerent, that it would cause much pain and upheaval. To this point, many of the river folk would leave the valley to its battle. This is the story of one such battle. This is how a fairytale grows up.

There was a young Passion of immeasurable beauty named Honeysuckle Sycamore. He was named this because he had been manifested under a honeysuckle-adorned sycamore tree while two young lovers consummated their adoration for one another beneath it. Born of their love, he was christened by the dew of the early morning. He stretched, yawned, and hopped to his feet as naked as a newborn. From his head hung a garland of honeysuckles and from his glittering skin came the scent of the sweet flower.

Honeysuckle was a joyous sprite, finding awe in everything he came upon. Hummingbird or grain of sand, it was all magnificent to him. The river folk gazed upon him with delight and reciprocated his laughter with giggles of their own.

Of all the sprites in the valley, Honeysuckle's most favorite – his absolute favoritest in all the wide world (which to him was a long flowing river and the hills above it) – was Dogwood. Dogwood liked nothing more than to sit beneath his trees and let the pretty white buds fall on him. He loved how they tickled his skin like kisses. His hair was a mussed bushel of white flame. Yet his skin was sun-kissed and dark.

Dogwood and Honeysuckle would play all day and all night by the river and among the thick trees of the forest. They would wrestle and kiss and romance the day away. Such was the free and gleeful existence of a Passion and river sprite. Many a human was envious of their frivolity.

One perfectly pleasant evening Honeysuckle and Dogwood skipped along the shore of the river, keeping awake the denizens of the valley with their laughter and guffaws. When they were shooed away by a rather gruff and particularly surly woman ("Git on witcha!" she squawked), giddily they ducked into a narrow hollow neither night fly nor hoot owl frequented. Their glee was quickly replaced by trepidation, however, as they journeyed farther inward. Their bare feet toppled the small pebbles and wet rocks of the hollow floor.

"Let's leave," Honeysuckle implored, pulling Dogwood's arm. "I do not like it here! Not one bit."

"Hush," Dogwood said, paying no heed to his friend's advice. "Do you hear that? Something is crying."

And sure enough, Honeysuckle heard the rasping, muffled cry. It was as if something were struggling to hold on to its last breath. It was a whinnying, shrill sound.

"Let's not go any farther," Honeysuckle said again, as quietly as he could.

"Quiet, Honeysuckle!" Dogwood commanded, adamantly. "It's just up a bit. Why not see what it is? Maybe we might help it if it be a deer or a lost stallion. We might ride it out of the hollow if it's not too distressed."

The narrow walls of the hollow led them to a dead end, a high cliff that shot into the night sky like a giant of the kind they had envisioned in one of their varied imaginary adventures.

"Look there!" Dogwood exclaimed.

At the base of the cliff, now silent and still, lay the form of a woman. Her white gown was fanned about her like wings about to take flight. Sitting beside her weeping was a young man with a bloodied knife in his hand. The blood dripped from it like molasses to the mossy rocks. He looked at the two sprites, imploring sympathy. "She had found another," he wailed. "She was going to leave me."

He looked despondent. Lost of all life and completely aware of the hopelessness of his situation.

"Brother, what should we do?" Honeysuckle gasped. His sweet breath tickled Dogwood's elfin ears.

Dogwood hadn't the time to answer, however. In a flash of confusion, they saw the young man plunge the dagger deep into his own chest. He gasped with a gurgle and a squeak, then fell back on the stony ground.

Honeysuckle and Dogwood clutched one another tightly. "Let us be gone!" Honeysuckle once more exclaimed. His voice sounded frail throughout the hollow.

Eric Arvin

As he said this, a deep, moaning pitch issued forth from the ground surrounding the dead couple. The two Passions stared around in fear. From the earth, from the moist ground rose at first a shadow. But as moonlight flooded the hollow, it became a great quivering hulk of naked flesh bathed in the blue glow of twilight. A Passion had been birthed. And it was one born of such jealousy and vile contempt that the sense of it began to permeate the valley almost immediately. An air of hate woke even those river folk who could sleep comfortably through the strongest summer storm. They sat straight up in their beds as if poked in the ribs with a fork and began to think of ways to leave, places to go.

The newborn Passion focused its coal-black eyes upon the two much smaller sprites. He was an awesome sight, and his name was Peat Moss. On his head was an emerald crown of lichen. With massive steps, he walked over the dead couple. The hollow groaned as he came for Honeysuckle Sycamore and Dogwood.

II

PASSIONS have the speed of a hummingbird's beating wings if they need it. No human could ever hope to tame or capture one. But against another Passion, against one of their own, they haven't that advantage. And not every Passion is as whip-quick as the next. There are certain inequalities, one might say. It all depends on the strength of the moment in which they were created.

As Peat Moss strode with dangerous intent ever closer to Dogwood and Honeysuckle, the two sprites lit into the forest air, their feet barely touching the smooth rocks of the hollow floor. Though Peat Moss was certainly a larger and more cumbersome-looking Passion than the other two, this in no way impeded him. So bitter, damp, and cold was his essence that Honeysuckle and

Dogwood at once felt his shadow over them as they fled like a coming winter storm.

They burst free of the hollow as mere glimmers of light that any watching human would think but plays of moonlight on the river valley air. Honeysuckle was always the faster of the two sprites and in no time, propelled by fear, had sped on ahead of Dogwood. It was only when he heard Dogwood cry out that he finally realized they were no longer together.

He turned to see the giant, newly born Passion dragging Dogwood by his lustrous white hair along the sand to the river. Dogwood kicked and hit as hard as he could, flailing about like a fish on a hook, but his blows were mere tickles to Peat Moss. Finally, having tired of Dogwood's struggle, Peat Moss leveled a shattering blow of his own against the young sprite. At once, Dogwood was dazed.

"Dogwood, no!" Honeysuckle exclaimed. He stood breathless for a moment, fear rendering him to stone. "Get up! Get up!" he thought. "Fight, Dogwood!" But seeing his companion incapacitated and sensing the true danger, the thought occurred to him: What would Honeysuckle do without Dogwood?

Quietly, with as much stealth as he could, Honeysuckle crept closer to the river's edge. From behind a boulder he spied as the giant beat the young sprite with merciless force. The expression on Peat Moss' face was one of devious delight; a crippled grin dripping with drool lay like a scar across his face. He grunted like a wild boar as he swung again and again. Defenseless, Dogwood took the blows and was soon limp even as Peat Moss continued his relentless barrage.

Honeysuckle did not need to wait long for his courage to mount (a strange, new sensation to him, for it had never been needed before). He sped at the behemoth as if his feet were lit by flames, tearing across the valley air with haste. Though he hit Peat Moss with unbridled force, it did little to lessen the monster's attack on Dogwood. With the effort of a shrug from Peat Moss, Honeysuckle was thrown off, slamming forcefully against the boulder. Before Honeysuckle lost total consciousness, he made a final attempt to rise and rescue Dogwood. But it was futile. His body, like Dogwood's, was as limp as river weed.

"I'm sorry, Dogwood," he whispered as his eyes closed on the night.

WHEN a Passion dies, it disperses into a thousand pieces carried away by the breeze like dandelion seeds. There is no body or shell left behind to bury or weep over. There is no grand funerary procession. Yet like everything of substance and energy the essence of the Passion remains in the world until a time comes that it may be reborn.

When Honeysuckle awoke, the light of dawn was breaking upon the shore. The patch of beach where Dogwood had fallen was bare, and only a dozen or so dogwood petals fluttered in the breeze. They circled, chasing one another as if ignorant of the death of a Passion. When a stronger breeze came and snatched them quickly away Honeysuckle jumped to his feet as if trying to catch them. But they were carried higher in the sky and far up stream. He lost sight of them in the blinding glare of the new day's sun.

Defeated and despairing, Honeysuckle slumped to the ground and wept. His hands dug into the sand in angst. His tears fell, mingling with the sand and the vanishing remnants of Passion blood. "Dogwood! Don't leave your Honeysuckle!"

And as he cried, the wind kicked up around him, his moans seeming a call for creation. Wind, sand, blood and tears had taken form in a stationary twister conducted by howls of grief. When the cyclone finally abated and Honeysuckle sat broken and sobbing, behind him stood a figure. A female energy born of sand

and bitter anguish. She swayed back and forth in plaintive, half-crazed repetition. Her name was Grit.

III

So consumed was Honeysuckle by his grief that he did not notice the swaying figure behind him. Only little by little did he differentiate between his utterances of grief and the long, queasy moans of the newborn female sprite. When at last he did comprehend he was not alone, he rose in surprise with a sudden leap.

"Who are you?" he demanded, the words barely finding a path through his sadness.

She did not respond. She rocked slowly, and her arms and neck moved in a delicate, mournful choreography. She was unlike anything he had ever come upon. Her flesh was porous and granular.

Where her eyes should have been were pits which cried constant, thin streams of sand. And her groans of grief issued forth from a mouth that was tightly, painfully clenched.

"Who are you?" Honeysuckle said again with a mingling of fear and pity. Instinctively, he reached for her as if he would touch her face.

As he did this, she quieted instantly and came toward him like a child taking its first, wobbly steps. He recoiled at once and fled into the forest, not looking back. While Honeysuckle was much quicker than Grit (he had left her behind on the beach in no time), the loss of Dogwood had slowed him considerably. Heartbreak weighed him down, and he soon found rest upon a hill within a thicket of briars and vines, wondering what other horrors awaited him.

Honeysuckle was quite content to lie in the thicket, to fade away like so many other Passions had done before him once their

strength had waned. He was finding desperate comfort in the darkness of closed eyes. If only he could rid himself of the stubborn consciousness that clung to him so obsessively.

A shuffling in the forest down the hill woke him from his black contentment long before he heard the accompanying moans. He looked through the leafless, dead thicket he lay beneath and perceived the female sprite as she staggered toward the hill. She stood at the base, her face tilted upward, her hands gesturing an embrace in lyrical dance. She tried to climb the hill, but was unable to traverse the steep incline. Immediately, she stumbled, falling to her knees. Moaning anew from the ground, she peered up at Honeysuckle.

"Go away!" Honeysuckle cried. "I do not know you! I do not want you." Yet, as he said it, he knew there was something in the tortured sprite down below that was all too familiar. "Go away, Grit," he said, knowing her name as easily as any being would innately recognize its kin.

But she didn't go away; she remained. And in her remaining was Honeysuckle's deliverance from nonexistence. Even as he had wanted to disappear, to vanish completely, the image of Grit waiting for him at the base of the hill kept him preoccupied. Her need for him was driving his need to die further from his mind.

Days and nights passed and neither of the two moved from their positions. Every morning Honeysuckle would wake to see Grit still at the bottom of the hill, still waiting and moaning plaintively. Every day his cries of resentment toward her became less forced. At last, he thought of coming down the hill. He was hungry, and he knew she had to be as well. But reluctance won out, and he remained in his fortress of dead vines for another night.

As he slept that night, Honeysuckle wandered into a dream: He slid down the hillside to where Grit lay slumbering. She grumbled and kicked like a dreaming hound. The imposing trees barely gave the moonlight admittance to the forest. As Honeysuckle watched the sleeping Passion, tendrils of honeysuckle began to climb delicately over her. And behind her a small tree sprouted from the forest floor. Both the honeysuckle vines and the tree grew very quickly, many seasons in only a few seconds. When the sudden growth stopped, Grit lay covered in a blanket of honey ivy and cradled lovingly by a large dogwood tree.

There was movement in the darkness of the forest beyond which distracted Honeysuckle from his adoration of Grit.

"Dogwood!" he gasped as he saw the certain form of his beloved walking away. Dogwood turned and grinned with a nod to Grit before fading into the night of Dreamland.

Honeysuckle woke to the morning, tears dripping from his cheeks like dew. He knew then he was not meant to suffer through his sorrow alone.

As in the dream, Honeysuckle slid down the hillside, though now in the clear light of morning he could see perfectly. So quick was his descent, he nearly fell on Grit as he approached the bottom of the hill. She was still sleeping. He watched her momentarily, still somewhat scared.

"Grit," he whispered, extending his hand and this time not recoiling. "Wake up, Grit. I'm here for you now."

Grit rose with a twitch, and turned her head about as if trying to see. The sand dripped from her face in heartbreaking streams.

"Grit. It's me. It's Honeysuckle Sycamore."

She moaned quietly with a strain of uncertainty, then made another attempt to embrace him with a lurch, a lunge, and a fall into Honeysuckle's waiting arms. She whimpered and sobbed there, at least minutely comforted.

"I'm here, Grit. It's you and me now." He held her closely for the rest of the day. The forest had never seen such brokenheartedness. Every willow in the vicinity wept at once and continues weeping to this very day.

They both retreated like fading shadows swallowed by the deep forest of the valley. The sheen of the world that Honeysuckle had known had dulled. There was no mirth or wonder left. Honeysuckle and Grit became but omens of grief and solitude to whatever soul they came across.

In the evenings, when light struggled through the trees and a cool breeze crept over the hillsides, they made their beds in tree hollows and sinkholes. Honeysuckle would hold Grit like an older brother or a concerned parent. In holding her, he perceived there was something about her that didn't quite fit. That is, though she was of Dogwood and Honeysuckle, something in her being was neither of them.

When Grit moaned and rocked in her sleep it would break Honeysuckle's heart. And it was during these moments that Honeysuckle would smell the faintest hint of Dogwood in the air and would know his beloved was still near watching over them both.

IV

FOR the most part, the valley had been abandoned. A perceptible darkness could be felt by those humans who lived there, a presence much darker and dangerous than any they had ever felt before. So, they fled from it. The valley itself grew hushed, its beauty hiding something jagged and sharp just beneath the tranquil surface. There were a few brave souls who remained; those who were simply too stubborn to leave or who chose to fight the bitter air alongside the energies of the earth. But they were scattered the length of the river, their homes tucked and hidden in the bends and curves of the valley.

Jess Bethel was a young man of nature. He was raised in the woods by an elderly monk and would have been a monk himself if there had been a monastery nearby to take him after the old man died. He wore a simple brown robe which covered a strong body sculpted by years of manual labor. He resided deep in the forest in the remains of the old, stone chapel that had been his aged, adopted father's home.

Honeysuckle Sycamore stumbled upon Jess as the young monk collected water from one of the creeks that streamed from the hills into the river. As he gathered the water into an old bucket, the long limbs of a dogwood tree stretched over him, and its petals sprinkled around him like a blessing. Something of Honeysuckle's old awe returned to him upon seeing Jess, and he could not help but follow the young man back to the chapel. The monk of course knew he was being observed and would often stop and wait when Honeysuckle, slowed by Grit's measured progress, would fall behind. And try as he might, Honeysuckle could never get Grit to remain completely silent. ("Hush, Grit! We do not want to scare him away.")

That first evening Honeysuckle and Grit hid outside the ruins of the old chapel with the crickets and hoot owls. The light from a single candle lit the interior. What Honeysuckle was waiting for, or why he had dragged poor Grit along, he couldn't say. He was enamored by Jess Bethel. He thought him the most magical being he had seen since his dear Dogwood. The sprite's eyes were once again wide with delight.

As the dusk light settled on the valley hills, the monk came to the chapel door and placed bread, berries, and fresh tomatoes on the moss-grown, stone walkway. He then turned and walked back into the chapel with nary a look behind.

"Look there, Grit!" Honeysuckle whispered excitedly. "The young human has left food. Do you think it's for us, Grit?"

Grit said nothing. She only moaned softly and cried her sand tears as she wrapped her arms around him.

"You just sit here, dear Grit," he said. "I think he does indeed mean it for us. What a kind, kind man!" Honeysuckle then darted out of hiding, quickly collecting the food and bringing it back to his charge faster and more graceful than a leaping stag.

Jess Bethel watched quietly from within the chapel. His eyes twinkled, and he smiled with adoration at the Passion's innocence.

TIME passed, leaves changed, and though the memory of Dogwood was ever present, merriment at last returned to Honeysuckle Sycamore. At night, staring beyond the tree limbs at the sky he would whisper, "How has Honeysuckle survived without Dogwood?" He could not answer his own question, but he knew both Jess and Grit had parts to play in its truth. He avoided the river, though. He knew he could never again play along its banks, never enjoy its sway or song. Not until Dogwood returned or until all Passions had died and there was never any use for rivers at all. In his life in the forest, Honeysuckle Sycamore had become a caged Passion.

Grit remained forlorn, as was her nature. She was born of the darker tendencies, after all. No matter what Honeysuckle did or what gifts Jess brought her, she gave nothing more than a grunt in reply.

"Poor Grit," Honeysuckle sighed, catching a grain of sand as it fell from her eyes. "Won't you ever smile?"

As the seasons took turns cradling the valley, a quiet romance flowered beneath the canopy in the old, stone chapel. The silent monk and the Passion became very much captivated with one another. They slept tenderly in each other's arms, they gathered berries and firewood, they bathed one another in the stream, and they cared for the lost child, Grit. Theirs was a happy, silent, shrouded existence.

When Honeysuckle and Jess Bethel made love for the first time, it was as if the purity of the valley had at last returned. The forest around them took on the quality of Truth, a wind of fresh understanding. Even Grit noticed the change as she slept in her bed of leaves on the forest floor. It was enough to quiet her grief-calls and still her incessant rocking, lulling her to her first peaceful rest.

The young monk had never known the world to be as beautiful or as shining as it was the moment a caged Passion came into him. Honeysuckle's love was like a tree sprouting inside Jess. Branches of joy spread out from the spot the seed was planted and grew through the monk's veins making everything more vibrant and filled with life, indestructible. From that day on, everything held a much higher quality for Jess Bethel.

As Honeysuckle came into him and they were joined, the sprite's laughter and glee filled the air. It eased through the forest, wrapping around the trees and traipsing down the hillside, until it finally came to the river where it swam gracefully along the current.

Down river something less beautiful had transpired, however. A trail of smashed pulp and smeared blood littered the banks, remnants of a small massacre. Peat Moss stood on the rocks, ripping apart what was left of a gaggle of geese he had come across. As a Passion he could easily overtake any flying creature. With the geese he had only to open his large arms to catch them all in a deadly embrace. Feathers, blood, and guts stained his face, hands, and chest. And when there was nothing left alive or twitching, he grimaced in disappointment. His blood lust could never be satiated. He wanted more – more blood, more maiming, more death. He stomped and grunted in agitation.

Yes, he was quite irritable. That is, until his keen sense of smell perceived the scent of Honeysuckle, and his ears caught the slightest air of gaiety. His eyes lit up with the memory of a familiar (if long thought dead) acquaintance. Across his face crept the very same crippled grin he had worn the night he had been born in that narrow hollow. The scent of Honeysuckle gave him his first twinge of nostalgia. It was spiked with thorns.

Immediately, he dropped the mangled remains of his feast of fowl and tramped off up river, following the sweet scent of an ivy flower. The earth shook in his wake. He had work to do. There was some fun to be had out of a job only half finished.

V

PEAT MOSS had only known the pang of regret but once. And that particular experience had been an anomaly that startled him to his festering core. He had successfully pushed it back in his mind, shrouding it with more satisfying, grisly images. So, as he leaped and bounded up river following the scent of honeysuckle flowers, his mind was unfettered by remorse.

Still, the hidden memory hung in the air, just above his head. If it were a rain cloud it might have burst at any moment. Within that burst, the only glimmer of decency Peat Moss had ever known would be released, and there could be no amount of denial that would keep it from pouring down upon him....

FOLLOWING his birth in the narrow hollow, Peat Moss had spent a good amount of time terrorizing the valley. He had nearly butchered, mangled, and maimed everything in sight, occasionally letting something flee so that it could be butchered, mangled, or maimed on another day. He was intoxicated by his own rage and brute strength. Nothing could control it.

Then, one day, Peat Moss caught a glimpse of Buford Longpost. Buford was one of the few who refused to leave the valley. He was a woodsman, sawing and selling timber to any who needed it and had made a name for himself among the valley folk. It was a name he was not going to give up without a fight. He spent most days felling the forest in anticipation of the return of life to the valley. Against his will, Peat Moss was immediately and inexplicably fascinated by the man. Buford was the strongest human Peat Moss had ever seen. His muscles shone bathed in sweat beneath the glare of the sun as he worked. Such strength on a human was dazzling to the Passion. Buford swung his axe so hardily that entire tree stumps were split in two with one mighty blow.

Peat Moss could not describe the feelings surging through him. He had no vocabulary for it, nor any precedence for any such feelings before. It frightened him that he felt such strong emotion toward this man, and that fear frightened him all the more. He had never before known fear, either. But he sat hidden by the trees in uncharacteristic awe and watched the lumberman whopping on wood the whole morning through.

At midday, Buford ate lunch and afterward stripped off his sweat-laden clothing, letting the sun's rays stroke his naked flesh. Peat Moss felt his very first hint of sexual desire. This was a day, it seemed, profuse with firsts. Buford stretched out upon a fallen tree, his head resting on his arms and his feet crossed at the ankles. His penis towered high in the air, seeking attention. It wasn't long before Buford's hand obliged the virile organ. With his eyes closed, he carried a private fantasy to fulfillment. When finished, he turned on his stomach satisfied and quickly fell asleep.

Peat Moss was flustered by what he had seen and all the more intrigued by the strong man. His lustful Passion eyes ran along the napping form of the man. They took in every muscle and dimple until at last they came to a full stop on the woodsman's muscular, perfectly rounded ass.

Buford didn't stir from his rest as Peat Moss came finally out of hiding. Strangely, there was nothing for the lumberman to fear even if he had awoke. Peat Moss wanted nothing more than to touch him and hold him. These very thoughts disturbed the Passion even as he tried to beat them down. But it was of no use; he was completely awestruck by the woodsman. His large hands caressed and kneaded every curve on Buford's physique. Seeing that this did not disturb the timber man, Peat Moss did something he had never done before: he kissed the bare skin of Buford's broad back.

At the touch of lips to salty skin, Peat Moss felt his own penis stiffening, and something of his more familiar self regained control. He could contain his appetite no longer. He parted the large mounds of the woodsman's muscular ass and sunk into him. Buford groaned, but it was not the kind of groan to which Peat Moss was accustomed. No, the woodsman sounded as if he didn't mind. Indeed, as if it were expected. As if his dreams at that very moment were one and the same with the reality of what was happening.

Buford ground himself back into Peat Moss, taking what he could of the Passion's ample member and causing the monster to thrust deeper. Peat Moss' sexual energy could have easily and literally ripped the man apart, but curiously, he did not wish for that. Something about this particular human had him under control. He found that he wanted to please him, not harm him, and that thought – the suddenness with which it came to him – was like a shock coursing from the woodsman's body into his own. The force of it caused him to tumble backward, rending his massive penis from the lumberjack's hole. This, of course, woke the lumberman quite forcefully from his sexual fantasy, and he looked around in surprise. At sight of the behemoth Passion, Buford fell from the tree and staggered aback.

"Keep away! Stay back!" he shouted, his voice deep and resounding. His face shone with terror.

Peat Moss was all too familiar with that expression. However, seeing it on the woodsman's face gave him an incomprehensible pang in his chest.

Peat Moss came toward the lumberjack. He would calm the man down, hold him. Then the woodsman would understand that they could be together; that he meant him – only him – no harm. They could fell flora and fauna as a mighty twosome. The river would run thick with blood and sawdust.

But Buford did not understand the approach, and suddenly lifted a large limb that lay near his feet, throwing it at the monster. Peat Moss swatted it away with ease and continued to advance. Buford pitched a stream of items at the Passion, all of them harmless. After a bit of this, Peat Moss began to think that the lumberjack was simply playing. After all, others who had caught sight of him immediately tried to escape. Yes. That was it. The woodsman was playing. They were having fun. Peat Moss grinned with delight and mischief at the realization he had a playmate and lifted from the earth the large tree Buford had been resting upon.

Buford had no time to move before the tree fell on him, crushing him into the ground. At once, Peat Moss' face fell. The human had not moved. Lifting the tree from the spot and peering down at the bloody mess of a man, the Passion howled. Why had the strong man not moved? The blast from the Passion's breath cleared the spot of any living thing, and all the fallen trees and cut wood were turned to ash.

But his mourning period was brief. For as he howled, the bitter winds began to kick up and a Passion began to form of his grief. This distraction irritated the monster so that at once he reached through the swirling mass of creation before the new

Passion had chance to fully form and bit its head off with a single chomp of his powerful jaws.

He put grief behind him, locking away the memory of Buford Longpost, and remained the Passion born of Darkness who terrorized the valley.

VI

IN the chapel, beneath the rotted thatched roof, Honeysuckle lay in Jess Bethel's arms. Their lovemaking had once again lasted the whole night through, causing the forest to emit an air of contentment and ease. As Honeysuckle embraced Jess in the night, a remarkable and somewhat frightening thing occurred. Whether it was a trick of the moonlight sneaking past the canopy of trees or a spark of dormant magic he could not say. But as they made love, the monk's face seemed to transform momentarily. Over the handsome human face appeared the visage of another. That of Dogwood. And he was grinning in absolute love. The kind of grin Dogwood had always given Honeysuckle whilst they lay entwined beneath the blossoming trees in their halcyon days.

AT first, Honeysuckle paused in alarm. "Dogwood?" he whispered.

But as soon as he spoke, the shadowed face of Jess returned, peering at the sprite with loving concern.

"Was nothing but a trick of light," Honeysuckle explained to himself, and he blessed the monk's face with fresh kisses.

AS morning broke, Grit wandered out of the cover of the trees and ambled onto the bank of the river. She had been emerging from the forest more and more of late, hearing the river as it passed her by. She would stand and moan along with its crystal song.

Her newfound independence did not go unnoticed by Honeysuckle and Jess.

"Why does Grit leave us now?" Honeysuckle wondered one morning as they ground grain for bread.

Jess shrugged and kissed the worry from the sprite's eyes.

Grit soon began to greet every sunrise by the river, and would often stay there into the early hours of the afternoon. At least until Jess would come and take her by the hand, leading her back into the safety of the woods. She would follow him without quarrel.

This particular day, however, Grit had reason to stand vigil at the river bank. Like a sightless sentinel, she did her macabre dance of sway, facing this way and that. She sensed something, some familiar and frightening presence in the air. Something intent on harm. She stumbled over the sand and rocks, here and there, trying to get a better sense of whatever it was that was coming. She was uncertain of its origins, but she knew she didn't like it one bit.

Behind her, the rustling of bare feet and dragging robe on the ground let her know Jess had come to retrieve her for their lunchtime picnic. Silent as ever, he stood, waiting for her to fumble toward him. She was slow in coming, though. Jess could see she was distracted. Grit continued spasmodically facing up then down river, moaning in unintelligible notes. She lurched her shoulders as if she were a cat among hounds.

When at last she did make her way to Jess, grabbing hold of his tattered robe, she was still quite tense and shaken. Jess led the way slowly through the forest path with Grit ever his token charge. He had come to view her with great affection, and her angst was extremely troubling for him.

As they left the riverside, delving farther into the forest, Grit became less agitated. Still, something was wrong. Upon catching sight of her at the chapel, Honeysuckle could tell as much.

"Grit," he soothed. "Why do you moan so? 'Tis a beautiful day, and see what tasty morsels we have to eat?" He raised a slice of warm bread slathered in thick raspberry jam.

Grit turned from the treat, tearing herself from the comfort of family, and frantically rambled about the vicinity. She batted at bushes and trees, tore vines, and threw stones. Her cries reached a disturbing crescendo, higher than Honeysuckle had ever heard. The cry curled the color off green leaves.

"Grit!" Honeysuckle exclaimed. "What's the matter?" He looked to Jess for a possible explanation, but the monk could only shrug in puzzlement.

Grit reached with both arms into the harmless forest air, as if grabbing at something directly in front of her. She looked like she might rip the world asunder. For the first time, she exhibited something resembling anger.

Honeysuckle came to her, wrapping his arms about her and pulling her back to the chapel. He and Jess comforted her even as her fit continued. Even as she lifted her face to the sky and screamed in blatant rage and the hillside seemed to shudder in dismay.

BEYOND the view of the Passions and the monk, hidden by the bramble of the woods, two eyes watched intently, contemptuously. Peat Moss only recognized the form of Honeysuckle Sycamore. The human could be easily dealt with. But it was the female sprite that caused the monster to stall his rampage that he had intended to unleash upon them. Something about her, something within her, shook him to the core for only the second time in his entire existence.

VII

IT was with much anxiety that Honeysuckle at last returned to the river. Grit had been so shaken upon her return to the chapel, neither he nor Jess could calm her. He needed to know what she had discovered, what had frightened her so. Some instinct in him wanted to protect her.

He approached the river with fear edging on disgust. He sat hidden by the trees for some time and watched the river from the hillside. His eyes were fixed on it as if it were returning his stare and neither of them would forfeit and break the battle of gazes.

Finally, though, Honeysuckle's fierce concern for Grit won out, and he broke through the trepidation that had caged him for so long. He stepped quickly from the forest to the beach, and it was as if a breakwall had given out. Upon him cascaded and swirled all the goodness the river had given him. He realized how much he had missed the banks and the sound of water. Yes, there was immense pain there. But there was also undeniable joy.

HE waded into the shallowness at river's edge, feeling the water embrace him again. And as he looked into the river his own image changed in much the same manner as Jess had seemingly transformed before his eyes the night before. Now, instead of his own reflection, Dogwood peered back at him once more, now in the clear light of the day. Dogwood raised his powerful arm from his side and placed it palm-up toward Honeysuckle. In tears, Honeysuckle did the same, mirroring the mirror. As his hand lay over Dogwood's palm, the water rippled and the glassy image became that of Jess. And then it shuddered once more and

169

became Grit. Yet, it wasn't Grit. For there, in the water she seemed different...Content. Happy even.

"Loves of my life," Honeysuckle whispered, his tears adding to the flow of the current. "And you are with me."

THOUGH Grit had scared Peat Moss from instantly attacking Honeysuckle Sycamore at the chapel, it was not her presence alone that took the monster aback. As he hid in the brush watching the two sprites and their human he began to hear whispers. These whispers coincided with a strange tinge of jealousy he felt at observing the tenderness between Honeysuckle and the young monk. From the tops of the trees the intimations seemed to fall. Like mist around him they settled. They were barely audible at first, but then grew in strength. Peat Moss turned this way and that in startled watchfulness. He stumbled away from his hiding place, but the whispers followed him. He swatted at them like gnats, but they would not be silenced. Grunting and flailing, he ran through the forest and down the hillside until he came to a cave he had often taken refuge in during a storm. And at once, the voices hushed.

Peat Moss peered into the darkness. Though he could no longer hear the invasive whispers, he sensed something still clung to the air around him. He was not alone. He swung angrily, attempting to grab whatever creature had dared follow him into the cave.

He began to see tiny balls of light, like fireflies, only much smaller and faster. They took up the whispering again, but now louder. They whirled about him, over him. Try as he might, he could catch none of them. He growled in frustration, and it echoed off the cave walls.

Soon, the tiny orbs began to cluster into a single, larger orb. It then became a blinding white light at the center of the cave. Peat Moss shielded his eyes from its brilliance. And slowly the giant orb began to take form, and the angered whispering suddenly dispersed again. Peat Moss' eyes widened in pain and regret as the ghostly vision of Buford Longpost formed silent and aglow in front of him.

VIII

JESS Bethel naturally cared for the woods and river as well as all the critters of the forest with unswerving felicity. He loved the sprites of the Valley, too, especially Honeysuckle Sycamore. He even adored Grit, for he could see past the bitter hurt and distorted pain that made her continuously weep and gnash her teeth. He saw in her a soul bound by ropes of grief. To Jess, all manner of creation was part of the great miracle.

His gentle nature, though an inherent thing among most creatures, was imprinted on him more so by the kindness that was shown him during his earlier years, a kindness that began when he was a newborn child. His origins were unknown to the individual who eventually found him floating like a bible story hero upriver in a shoddy wicker basket. Brother Patricio Bethel was a very old man. He had outlived anyone that anybody in the valley had ever known. He was thinner than a cattail cane, and his long robes hung from him like linens out on the line set to dry. The children of the valley found him particularly strange and could not help but stare on the odd occasion that they saw him. Brother Patricio walked on all fours. This was due to a bone disease he had developed in early life that had never been corrected. The truth is, however, he had never thought about it too much. It never seemed much of a malady to him. His soul had a greater purpose.

When the old monk found the lost baby floating among the reeds as quiet and calm as if the river itself were its mother, he at once took charge of the child. He cradled and fed it, and as the boy grew, taught him the ways of the valley. Young Jess

Bethel was ever the dutiful son and was content in his world of the stone chapel with Brother Patricio. They made their bread and wine, they tended to the forest and its inhabitants, and they comforted the people of the valley when the people needed comforting. They never wandered too far from the chapel's crumbling walls.

Even the Passions of the valley found the chapel a wonderful playground, and Brother Patricio always enjoyed watching his adopted son play among them. Jess seemed more inclined to the wonders of the sprites than the growing cynicism of the valley children.

Things continued blissfully until Jess Bethel was a young man. One day, while mixing dough for a wheat bread, the old monk fell over and died. It was as simple as that. There were no long illnesses or deathbed farewells. Jess buried Patricio beneath the roots of an oak tree near the chapel and continued to look after the old place even when the valley folk had long since forgotten it was there. And so that is where he remained until that day when a curious sprite in mourning followed him home.

PEAT MOSS stared steadily into the dark of the cave. If there remained a brave soul left in the valley and they chanced past the opening, they would have seen the Passion hunched and as stoic as a statue, peering glassy-eyed at the cave wall. But Peat Moss saw something there no passer-by could have seen. His grief had overcome him. The ghost of Buford Longpost, the only being for which Peat Moss had ever felt any affection, glared back at him. He was an unmoving spirit; as fixed to his spot as Peat Moss.

The Passion's defeated eyes almost cried true tears. He almost wept bitterly at the memory of Buford's demise. But then something transpired that prevented that. One by one, ghost by ghost, the whisper had spun through the afterworld that the angry Passion's eyes were open and he could see spirits. Those beings that Peat Moss had massacred and murdered began to trickle slowly into the cave out of curiosity and a taste of vengeance. It was only a small stream of lost consciousness at first. But it soon became a deluge. It wasn't long before the sprite saw around him the glaring, angry faces of everything he had ever killed. And they were not as quiet as the silent woodsman's ghost. No, they were bitter and resentful, shouting and moaning. They tried their best to reach out from the eternal divide and drag him into their world so that they might each in their turn rip him asunder.

This cavalcade of anger brought Peat Moss back to himself. He felt the hate and ire that was his life's purpose return to him. At once, he rose and clamored after the spirits, wanting to kill them all over again. But he could not reach into their world, either. Yet the angry calls of the ghosts still harassed him.

Exasperated, Peat Moss ran from the cave. He realized he could not defend himself from the calls of ghosts. But still, the victims of his malevolence followed him, torturing him through the woods; an army of the dead searching for bloody closure.

In his flight from the cave, Peat Moss had unknowingly exposed his whereabouts to an investigatory Grit. Still perturbed by the sense of unease that wrapped around her heart, she had gone wandering through the forest yet again. Her intent was to find the source of her mysterious restiveness and put an end to it. Though how that was to happen was a mystery to her.

Grit heard the ruckus and determinedly made her way in the direction of the cave. It took some doing. She fell more than once. But eventually she found it. And while Peat Moss was long gone, his mind slowly being chipped away by the voices of the dead, she felt his essence of hate. She ran her fingers over the cave walls, picking up his scent. It was then she realized what she had to do. She understood who this abhorrent creature was; what he meant to her. So, she walked from the cave and slowly felt her way back to the chapel.

IX

A lost bumble-bird was perched on the branch of a dogwood tree near the abandoned settlement that once thrived with the valley folk. The tiny creature had been out all day collecting pollen and twigs, but had wandered too far from its hive. Now the squat little fellow thought it best that he settle somewhere and get his bearings.

He looked around at the dilapidated houses with their falling roofs and overgrown lawns. For a bumble-bird this was a prime twig-collecting area. His surroundings were silent. Only the river made any noise, its flow clearing obstacles from the little creature's mind. Maybe he would be able to remember his way home.

The quiet and still was not long lasting, however. From upstream came a gentle sloshing through the shallow edges of the river. It was a Passion, the first the bumble-bird had ever seen in his short life. For the valley had been abandoned of any such spirits for quite some time. Long before this little bumble-bird had been hatched in the hive.

He looked curiously at the beautiful sprite that was Honeysuckle Sycamore. And, of course, the Passion noticed the bird at once and gleefully spoke to it.

"Hey, bird," Honeysuckle said. "I haven't been here in such a long time. Are you new here? Or is this your tree now? Is that your branch? Though, I don't suppose it matters. All the people are gone. You have your pick of branches and trees. But I have a feeling, bird. I have a feeling they're all going to come back, and very soon. What do you say to that, bird? Wouldn't it be nice to sleep in pumpkin patches again?"

The bumble-bird cocked its tiny head. Soon the sprite walked on, looking through the homes and gardens with hungry wonder. The bird watched for a bit, then, after remembering a

174

certain tree and its proximity to the hive, he flew in the direction of the hillside.

He flew into the forest, gliding on a sweet breeze, until he again could not recognize his surroundings. So, again, he alighted upon a limb. Below him, struggling through the dense wood over large roots and hills was the strangest creature the little fella had ever seen. Stranger still then the sprite Honeysuckle Sycamore. This sprite was tortured and sad. She twitched and spasmed as she made a slow progression through the forest. Still, she was clearly on a mission. There was a direction to her chaotic journeying. It was as if she held a scent and was following it with an unalterable intent, tearing down limbs and plowing through mounds of leaves that stood in her way. What purpose, the little bird could not tell. But it headed off in the same direction. Perhaps where she was headed was where he needed to be as well.

The bumble-bird flew past the sprite Grit until she could no longer be seen. Soon he came upon the most fearsome of all the things he had yet seen that wondrous day. A large, angry Passion was batting at the air wildly, and grumbling and moaning in crazed gestures. The bird had to fly higher to avoid being smashed to a pulp by the massive strength of the monster. He did not stay long in that area of the wood. He flew on away, but now in the direction of the angry Passion's trek.

At last, the little bumble-bird recognized some of its own hive mates sitting upon the rotting roof of a little chapel and he flitted off to join them. He buzzed and tweeted happy hellos at the relations and spoke in birdspeak what he had seen on his journey. The other bumble-birds were amazed. They had all heard of Passions from the bumble-bird elders, but, the hive being so much farther up on the hillside, they had never actually seen one. And they weren't so certain they wanted to see this angry-looking Passion seen headed toward the chapel.

Down on the ground, a young monk watched them with apparent appreciation. The bumble-birds told their lost hive mate how wonderful the human was and how he adored them. He gave them crumbs of bread and sweet water. They all agreed that they should remember the way back to the chapel. Fearing the crazed monster, however, they flew away, the little lost bumble-bird as well, for their hive.

X

PEAT MOSS could not rid himself of the ghosts. They raged at him from all sides, dragging over him like transparent branches as he ran through the forest. Their screams and hollers of madness grew louder as he leveled tree and brush up the hillside. Ahead of him, sneaking in and out, from behind this tree then that, Peat Moss caught glimpses of the stoic spirit of Buford Longpost. The dead man's apparition would glance sidelong at him with an unchanging expression of indifference. As if Peat Moss were beyond his care, unimportant. The monster followed him, altering direction to wherever Buford had last appeared.

Jess Bethel was unaware of the monster's approach. Of his chase to catch Before Longpost and his own sanity. The young monk was in the yard of the chapel preparing to bring the day's water from the creek. Rampaging Passions being the furthest thing from his mind, he thought it was but another beautiful day in the valley forest.

There were hiccups, of course, in the beauty of the day. Every day had unexpected bumps. Grit had wandered off again in another frenzied, enigmatic search, and Honeysuckle had ventured to the river. This surprised Jess the most. The peaceful Passion it seemed had at last conquered his fear of the waters.

The strange changes in his family's behavior were not lost on the monk. He could sense something; a change in the winds of the world. But how that change might affect him, he did not know. How could one give a face to gravity if they never knew it existed? Jess had been sheltered for so long a time that the outside world or any danger it wrought was simply not a bother. In fact, he had always felt secure in the forest by the chapel. He had known nothing but goodness, first from Brother Patricio, then from Honeysuckle. The only great change that had come along had been that of Honeysuckle, and that was a welcomed wind. One as sweet as the scent of jasmine.

But now, this new sense of change – there was something menacing about it. Even more menacing than a sky full of heavy clouds threatening floods. He thought to himself that Grit was perhaps right to be concerned. Still, what can one do against the unknown? Against what's yet to happen? So Jess continued about his day in normalcy and routine.

Behind him, as he reached for the water bucket from where it hung by the chapel door, Jess heard a ruckus such as he had never known. He turned quickly and saw to his amazement birds, squirrels, raccoons, and all manner of forest creature fleeing out of the bush as if being chased by a violent predator or great forest fire. The creatures flew, hopped, and scampered past him, disappearing again into the opposite flora.

Then with a crack like thunder, a great tree was struck apart and fell to pieces, the wood splintering in a myriad of directions. The seething mass of quivering muscle which stood in its place could be none other than the Passion Peat Moss. The very one Honeysuckle had mentioned on quiet, desperate occasions when he took to mourning. The forest seemed to shrink around him as he heaved and twitched and growled.

At first, neither of the two reacted. Jess simply stared with mesmerized fear and awe. Then, the monster's eyes seemed to transform from blind rage to a kind of glazed familiarity. Jess could not know that at that moment Peat Moss no longer saw him as a peaceful monk, but now perceived him as his lost Buford. He could not know that Peat Moss thought to take him back to the

177

cave and make love to him forever. All Jess saw was a crazed grin creep across the Passion's troubled face.

The monk began to retreat slowly backward to the chapel. But Peat Moss was on him at once. With one mighty swing the wall of the chapel tumbled to the ground, and Peat Moss threw the struggling monk over his shoulder. Jess kicked and hit, strenuously defending himself. Peat Moss was tired of the struggle now, though. The spirits still pecked at him with their cries and goads. To have this man, the one he saw as Buford Longpost, being contentious as well would not do.

He threw the monk to the ground and hit him, knocking him out. The blow was not a hard one by the monster's standards, but it was sufficient. Jess fell limp, and the Passion picked the man up again and disappeared into the woods.

XI

...INTO the pitch of the woods Peat Moss carried the unconscious monk, Jess Bethel. Into the pitch of the woods followed every manner of spirit and phantasm, their cries of anger growing louder in the monster's ears. He tried to block the wretched noise, covering one ear. In doing this, he let drop Jess' legs so that now the monk was being dragged through the forest. But Peat Moss was not about to let go of his prize. He still held him in a constricting grasp.

It was the appearance of a very real form, not an apparition, that halted the Passion's trek. In front of him stood Grit, arms treading the air as if it were reeds she was searching through. Her face was vexed; she knew she was right upon it. That scent, that wisp of treachery she had been following stood directly in front of her now. The sense of danger she had felt that morning by the river, indeed, the sense of dread and grief that made up her very being, had never been stronger than it was at this moment.

Peat Moss watched, Jess now being held by only one arm, as the blind sprite edged toward him. At the sight of her, he felt a curious kinship. He had known there was something of him in her. He felt her pain as an extension of his own self. He ventured forward, attempting to gain a close enough proximity as to touch her.

Grit was immediately aware of his hate, his impending icy admiration. Peat Moss' shadow crawled over her like a glacier imposing itself on an unsuspecting landscape. Grit recognized the scent of Jess, the pressure of his self in the air. He was not well. Her reaction was swift to this knowledge. With a cry that pierced through the spirits in the air, making them flee in fear, she shattered the frigid darkness that Peat Moss' shadow cast.

At once, he stepped back. Grit's shrill aching cry made him double over. He dropped Jess completely to the forest floor, clasping his ears. Grit lurched and stammered over her own fear as she made for where she knew the monster to be. Her cry of anguish continued, and she reached for the Passion with long fingers that could rip a hole in the atmosphere. He had never seen such ferocity, not even his own when mirrored in the river could compare.

Forgetting the monk where Grit now stood in some grand protective stance, Peat Moss fled into the woods with the spirits. He bellowed as his ears bled from the pain. Grit would have followed, but he had fled too quickly. So she returned her attention to the unconscious monk.

As soon as he heard Grit's wails ripping through the valley air, Honeysuckle was racing to her. Dust and long grass flew in his wake. He felt a sudden guilt for having let her go alone into the forest. What if she had wandered into a cleft or a hunter's trap? But then he realized the cry issuing forth from beneath the canopied hillside was not one of pain or fear. No, her wailing was like that of an animal on the hunt; an animal which, upon having caught its prey, was proclaiming victory before descending upon it. It made Honeysuckle shiver, and he ran all the faster. He could not even feel the slight breeze, the flood of scattered spirits, as he ran through them on his way to find Grit.

At last, he found her. She sat on the ground, holding Jess' head in her hands as she moaned. Once understanding Honeysuckle was near, she reached for him pleadingly, and he ran to her side and sank to the ground. He feared Jess was dead and quickly felt for his breath.

"He lives!" Honeysuckle cried in relief. He kissed Jess gently on the forehead where honeysuckle-scented tears had fallen. Grit clung to Honeysuckle's arm, her grip loosening once he had diagnosed Jess's condition.

Honeysuckle knew without asking what had happened. Only one thing, one force of nature, could cause him this kind of grief. He kissed Jess once again, but this time with adamant force on the mouth; a gesture like a promise. The young monk's dazed eyes opened. Honeysuckle handed the care of Jess back to Grit.

"You stay here, Grit," Honeysuckle demanded. "You watch after our Jess." He stood with as much purpose as he had ever done. "I have something to take care of."

Grit jerked as if she understood what Honeysuckle intended to do. She reached for him in an effort to stop him, but he was already gone.

As he trod downhill, Honeysuckle Sycamore made the forest supplicant. His determination, his anger, his will, made every bow bend. Honeysuckle Sycamore was set to destroy Peat Moss once and for all.

XII

IT was not hard for Honeysuckle Sycamore to find Peat Moss. The valley itself exposed the monster's agitated rassling in the shallow water of the river as the sound of it echoed and bounced off the hills. The vengeful spirits had once again descended upon Peat Moss after having scattered in fear of Grit's howl. They pecked and hammered mercilessly at him. Now there was no crossing back over to sanity for the giant, and this made his ferocity an even more dangerous thing.

He rolled about in the river, struggling with an unseen adversary. He did not at first see Honeysuckle standing on the river bank with a determined rage in his eyes. The glaze of spirits had hampered his sight. Without waiting for the monster to pounce first, the Passion leaped into the stirred waters, bounding onto Peat Moss in a lightning flash. He had not moved as fast since the night Dogwood had been killed. This moment held the same intensity, but now he was not retreating.

The action caught the monster off-guard, for he had never been confronted so. Honeysuckle knocked Peat Moss beneath the still churning current. It took all of the smaller sprite's strength to do so. Yet, Peat Moss rose almost immediately with a deranged roar, the water pouring from him as if he were a mountain rising from the sea. Honeysuckle could now see the spirits which soared over and around Peat Moss like a towering cyclone. Peat Moss charged at him, throwing Honeysuckle across the river like a feather being tossed about by the wind. He landed on the banks, dazed, but would not give up until Peat Moss was gone from the valley for good. He rose just in time to see the monster's red fire eyes glaring at him in lust and hate. But Honeysuckle was past fear. Something else took hold of him; that of the memory and hope of everything he had ever loved. Dogwood, Jess, Grit, the Valley, the River.

Near him, he found a shard of rock; an arrowhead used by the valley folk for hunting, left behind years ago. He challenged the monster again, and the monster accepted.

The immensity of Peat Moss would have decimated Honeysuckle on impact, and the smaller sprite knew this. So just as they were about to collide, Honeysuckle leaped into the air, grabbing one of the long lichen tendrils of Peat Moss' mane, and swung himself over and up until he was squat on the monster's backside. He slashed at Peat Moss, cutting him deep, drawing thick, black streams of blood. Peat Moss howled in discomfort and anger, struggling to reach for Honeysuckle. But Honeysuckle dodged and gashed at the massive hands.

The sprite reached around for Peat Moss' throat, trying to find its vulnerability. He grabbed the monster's mane, pulling out strands of lichen. Peat Moss' head tilted back in a hateful growl, leaving his throat an easy target. Honeysuckle drew the arrowhead across it, and though blood was drawn, the skin was too thick, too rough. And it was too late.

Peat Moss' large hand found the sprite's leg at last and pulled Honeysuckle over his head and into the river. There he held him, Honeysuckle struggling for air beneath the giant's hands. An enormous sense of gratification and arousal overcame Peat Moss. He no longer noticed the banshees and spirits that still tried to thwart him. He drove into Honeysuckle with his thick penis even as he continued to drown him, holding the sprite's head below water but his bottom up and open.

Honeysuckle flailed beneath the monster's hold, but it was of no use. His strength could never hope to match that of Peat Moss. He could no longer bear it, the pressure, the torturous need for air, the relentless pounding, and so let go. Let the euphoria come in. The lovely, terrifying euphoria. And as he did so he saw Dogwood in the water beside him. Lying on the river bed shaking his head, as if saying not to give up. But how could he win?

Then something happened. The monster released Honeysuckle, and Dogwood faded like a wisp with a twinkle in his eye. Honeysuckle rose with a gasp, choking up water and struggling to stand aright. He was prepared to be knocked about again by the monster, to be played with. Perhaps, tortured for hours before being eventually killed. But Peat Moss was no longer interested in Honeysuckle. He stood silent and still in the water, staring to the shore as if mesmerized. Even the spirits had quieted around him.

Honeysuckle had drifted a ways downstream. He spotted Grit on the shore. She walked unsteadily toward the river's edge, falling and thrashing as she came deeper into the current.

"Grit, no!" Honeysuckle cried. "Go home, Grit!"

But she did not listen. She didn't even move her head as if she had heard him. Her attention was on Peat Moss alone. She waded to him, and he waited for her. Honeysuckle tried to get to them, but hadn't the strength now to cross the distance. The current was too strong.

Soon Grit stood face to face with Peat Moss. He grunted in strange recognition of her, raising his hand for her face.

"Grit!" Honeysuckle screamed, struggling through the water toward them.

As Peat Moss touched Grit's face, her expression changed from one of aching sorrow to harrowing contempt. A moan, plaintive at first, then cresting to a high-pitched rage, filled the air. Honeysuckle covered his ears and stared in awe. The spirits fled, scattering like leaves. Peat Moss also tried to hide from her deafening cry, but she caught his arm, and he could not wrest it. Grit's slit of a mouth suddenly curled and grew until it was a large hollow hole in her face. And then, to both the horror of Peat Moss and Honeysuckle, it stretched further until its size was surreal, mismatched with her form. Her face disappeared until only a gaping chasm of mouth could be seen, inside of which was nothing but blackness.

Peat Moss struggled against her, but his strength was nothing now. He raged and hit at her, but it did no harm. Then with one sudden movement, like a wave overtaking a village, Grit came down upon the mighty monster, swallowing him whole. The waters stirred in the spot where he had stood.

"Grit?" Honeysuckle whispered.

She stood silent for a moment, her arms out from her sides as if she were a scarecrow hung. Suddenly, she began to heave and convulse. With a sickening gag she vomited forth the remains of Peat Moss into the river. Black liquid mess. Down the hiding spirits descended around her, picking at what remained of the monster. Feasting on him as he had done on them. They crowded around Grit, shrouding her to the point that Honeysuckle could no longer see her. He knew she was there, though, for he could still hear the sickening continuous regurgitation.

And then it all stopped.

The spirits scattered once more, content with their vengeance. Grit stood alone and worn out in the water. But as Honeysuckle came for her, something else happened. Everything about the Passion Grit began to soften and color. Parts of her seemed to melt away revealing a newer, fresher being. To Honeysuckle's astonishment, before him in the river now stood Grit, though devoid of sorrow. She had eyes, real eyes, and a beautiful, bright smile.

"Father," she said loud and sure to Honeysuckle Sycamore. Her first word began the change in the valley. Better things to come.

HONEYSUCKLE SYCAMORE and Grit nursed Jess Bethel back to health. Jess was dazzled and delighted by Grit's new self, and she delighted in doting on him the way he had on her. Jess giggled too at the tiny arguments Grit and Honeysuckle would get caught up in, like a father and child at times, other times like two adversarial playmates ("The sunflower is the prettiest flower!" "No! It's the honeysuckle!") When Jess was able, the three of them took walks through the lonely forest, admiring it in a way they hadn't been able to before. With new eyes and free of fear.

Soon after, the mood in the valley changed once more. The days became the stuff of yesteryear; sweetness and happiness and warm days. Forest creatures returned or came out of hiding and played openly on the banks of the river. Bumble-birds twitter-bussed through the air, and deer paraded through the shallow streams. Word soon reached the ears of the outside world that the valley had returned to its true form. The monster Peat Moss had been destroyed. And so, little by little, the valley folk began to return. They reclaimed their places by the River, renewed their love and appreciation for the valley. When they discovered how Peat Moss had been defeated, they brought gifts and food to the Passions in the chapel and even rebuilt the chapel itself, strengthening the walls and fixing the roof.

Though nearly extinct, new Passions were being born every day once the valley folk returned. Born from nothing but love and frivolity. Once again, Passions were being chased from pumpkin patches by broom-wielding matriarchs. Once again, a poor scarecrow went naked through the summer and into autumn. Honeysuckle had never been happier. He knew Grit would be leaving soon, that she would want to go out and adventure as any sprite would. But he chose not to think on that. He chose instead to think on what was right in front of him in the valley by the river. Jess Bethel, Grit, and, when the moon was just right and he peered just so into the river's current, his Dogwood.

moonburn

in the bed
he and i
tight < wrapped like the word
one hot
faulkner night when
crickets gave breathing lessons
giving voice
to humidity

bodies rushing red
red and pink
like porcupine readiness

the beautiful complexity
of being vague

everything rises
wet sweat glory under glow
flushed fevered hot
increasing the flow

increasing
and increasing
and increasing the likelihood of moonburn

Eric Arvin

Absurdity on Jasper Lane

DAVID and Terrence sat up the lawn chairs as usual in the front yard. Every afternoon, weather permitting, they would lie out under the sun with their trendy shades and square-cut swim trunks and drink themselves into the night. It was a cliché, of course, but they embraced it. The heat called to them and gave them the gift of deep tans. All of Jasper Lane, gossip-loving housewives and dashing young men in suits, expected it of them.

"You know you both look like every gay stereotype I think I've ever seen," Rick said as he prepared to wash his car, a cherry red Mustang, in the driveway. It was a nice day for it. It wasn't yet August, so the harshest heat was yet to come.

"Oh, blah!" David shot back. "Who cares?" He took a small sip from the margarita he held.

"You should be more like us," Terrence added. "Maybe you'd get a date."

Rick grinned and soaped up the car. But Terrence had a point. Rick hadn't been out on a date in forever, and it wasn't because he was less than attractive. He had, in fact, very striking features. He had chosen to go as a Roman centurion just last Halloween to Betsy Jones's party partly because it fit his look so well. And, like David and Terrence - *hell, like every gay man* - he went to the gym regularly. But the thing he did lack was the verve to actually act upon impulse. He let moments of possible intrigue flee from him. He was, for the most part, considered fairly dull by the gossips of Jasper Lane. They were always polite and kind to him, but he knew that his stories would never interest any of them. He was not sure if that was a positive or a negative. The only thing that he was certain of was that he had not found his name mentioned in the larger-than-life stories retold like punch lines at dinner parties and barbecues.

Terrence and David were more of the go-getter type. They were loved and their escapades legendary. There was hardly a night that there wasn't something going on...or someone going down. And they always seemed to get themselves in trouble for it. At that very same Halloween party last October, Terrence, hearing that a very hot and available UPS man was coming dressed as Batman, showed up in full Boy Wonder gear. At some point during the evening he managed to get his tongue ring caught on the Caped Crusader's Prince Albert and bat thong. The rest of the night was spent very carefully getting the mess sorted out. David even took pictures and used them as Christmas cards. Terrence hated him for exactly one day, and then they were the best of friends again. Betsy Jones, of course, loved it. It gave her party the wonderful spin of infamy.

"Get over here and relax!" Terrence said. "The show's about to start." He spilt a drop of drink on his chest, and David licked it off playfully. They both giggled like teenagers.

"The Show?" Rick asked. "Is that his name?"

"Honey, we don't know what his name is yet, but we'll find out. You wait and see."

The Show was a new addition to the neighborhood. A tall, dark-haired young man with an incredible physique. He jogged past the house at the same time every afternoon. All they knew of him, straight from the mouth of Becky Ridgeworth, was that he lived alone in Mr. Goodman's old house (a cat lover who found out a little too late he was *very* allergic to cats) and had just got out of the army, hence the body. He made every straight woman and gay man in the vicinity think of nothing more than the best gay porn. (Gay porn was, thanks to David and Terrence, a new favorite pastime for the ladies. Cassie Bloom, the grand dame of the neighborhood, was the first to hold a gay porn party complete with penis-shaped finger foods.)

Terrence and David joked something inaudible to Rick and then continued with their sipping and sun worshipping. Rick lathered up the Mustang and began to rinse it with the hose. He didn't fully want to be robbed of seeing *The Show*, though. He had seen the man jogging around enough to understand the attraction. The Mustang needed a wash anyway, and that was a good enough excuse to be outside with the two sloshed knuckleheads.

Suddenly, the temperature seemed to shoot up several degrees, and the flowers drooped from the heat.

"There he is!" David snickered excitedly, hitting Terrence with playful jabs.

Rick looked up quickly. Sure enough, there *The Show* went. Shirtless and sweating, each muscle seemed to twitch and flex as he ran. Rick swallowed in desire. In all probability, anyone who was watching the ex-military man (and there were many) saw him in the same slow-motion movement, pectorals bouncing in fleshy waves. He wore military shorts, green and cut well above the knees so as to give a better glimpse of the fine muscles in the legs.

David and Terrence panted and moaned not so discreetly.

"My lord, those legs!" Terrence said.

"My god, that chest!" David answered.

Rick glanced at them and grinned, then returned to his task. That was good enough for today. Maybe tomorrow he could come up with some other plan to guarantee him a show.

He turned off the hose and began wiping the car down. It was streaking a bit, but he would wax it afterwards as well, then go for a drive. He needed to get his niece a birthday gift still.

Maybe before that, though, he would give himself a shower with the hose to wash off the lust.

Behind him, suddenly, the giddiness and cackling of his two boozing housemates ceased. There was an odd quiet, as if someone was about to jump out and scream *"Boo!"* Rick turned around out of curiosity, and his heart leapt. There in front of him stood the army man with his brawny, muscular hands placed on his hips. A droplet of sweat fell from the handsome man's dark hair; hair that was just now beginning to grow back from its clipped military style.

"Hi," he said, breathing heavily. A gorgeous grin lay across his face. A face that was not as hard or stern as one might expect from a military man.

"Hi," Rick said, stunned. Terrence and David watched, mouths agape, from the yard.

"Nice car," the man said. "My name's James. I'd shake your hand, but I'm all sweaty."

"That's okay," Rick said. "I'm Rick. I'm all wet. A little sweat won't bother me." He held out his hand, and James took it.

"So, listen, Rick. I've seen you around...I've noticed you..." He was stumbling to say something. "What I mean to say – and bear with me 'cos I've been in the army, and it's been a while – but I've seen you around and...would you like to go do something?"

"Now?" Rick asked, though he knew perfectly well what James was asking.

"No. Some time, though."

"A date?"

"A date. Yes," James said. "I was planning on trying to strike up a conversation with you about the car and then gently slide into asking, but...I was nervous – am nervous – so I just thought I'd get it over with. So I'd know for sure right away, you know?"

"Uh, yeah. I'd love to. I'd like that very much."

"Good," James sighed. The relief cascaded from him. He began to walk slowly backward with a victorious grin on his face. "I'll come by later. We can set it up then."

"Sounds good," Rick said, smiling in return.

James turned around. Rick saw that his ass was clearly the best and most sculpted in the neighborhood, beating even Steve Jones, Betsy's husband, who secretly did gay-for-pay videos to pay for their heavy expenses. James ran on down the street, waving once back at Rick, and then jogging out of sight.

"You fucking bitch!" David said, as he and Terrence looked at Rick with glares of disbelief.

"He doesn't have to go anywhere," Terrence complained to David. "They come to *him*!"

"You're going to tell us everything that happens," David said. "*Everything*, Cinderella! Your stepsisters want to know."

"No way, boys," Rick replied. "This is going to stay quiet. You can't tell anyone. I don't want the whole neighborhood knowing."

"Too late," Terrence said as he raised his shades to see the portly figure of Becky Ridgeworth power-walking up the drive toward Rick, a look of curiosity on her plump face like a heat-seeking missile.

"Cassie Bloom probably already knows," David said. "You're the talk of Jasper Lane already."

"So, this it," Rick said to himself with a worrisome grin. "My ticket into absurdity."

"Absurdity on Jasper Lane" was the inspiration for Eric Arvin's comedy SubSurdity: Vignettes from Jasper Lane, *available through iuniverse.com.*

Gordy Helps Out

THE weight room smelled like men at Harry's House of Fitness. That's not to say it stank; it just had that scent that men naturally exude, like salt and dampness. Some would call it intoxicating.

Four young men, cocky regulars, strutted about as if they owned the free weight area. They were good-looking and fit, adamant about looking like their steroid-enhanced idols in the muscle mags they bought on a weekly basis. They talked and acted as if they were already on level with the great muscle beasts, at least in the gym, at least around one another. They flexed and posed for the admiring girls who watched from a safe distance at the cables or the Body Solid machines. They were the kings of the weight room, so they thought, as young men of their age are often prone to think. They were certainly louder, which to them meant exceptionally more committed to fitness. There were other men in the gym, other big men. But they were older men. At least in their late 30s, and while they were impressive, they didn't strut, they didn't preen. To the four, this meant they weren't as focused. The foursome pitied the older muscle dudes. The older muscle dudes tolerated the foursome.

The leader of the four, it seemed, was a young buffer named Jerry. Jerry liked to talk trash. If anyone threatened his dominance, he made it known he was none too happy. He was the largest of the four, the most muscular. Nice 18-inch biceps were flexed continuously from the time he would walk in to the weight room to the time he would walk out.

"Man, I had this chick last night," he was saying to his three brethren. "She wanted it bad. Nice tits and one hell of an ass. Damn!"

The guys whooped in appreciation. They had stories of their own to tell. Stories, mind you.

"Did you give it to her?"

"I bet you nailed her good!"

"Oh, I gave it to her all right! Up the ass first. Damn, it was hot! She kept screaming 'More! More! Harder!'" There his voice took on the caricature of a woman. "I gave her more. I tired her out, man. I tire all the ladies out."

Jerry noticed the guys had suddenly stopped listening to him. Their attention, indeed, the attention of everyone in the gym, was focused now on something else.

Into the weight room, barefoot, shirtless, massive, and innocently smiling, strode something neither Jerry nor his comrades had seen before at their gym. This 'something's' name was Gordy. Gordy was larger than any bodybuilder they had ever seen, but he was not beaten-looking. He didn't look bloated from steroid use. The guy looked completely natural, but that had to be an impossibility. All four of the guys' jaws dropped unwittingly.

Gordy wore but a tiny pair of green running shorts that stretched tight across his thighs, revealing a nice bulge in the crotch. Sighs were escaping from patrons all around him as he walked past. This was his first day trying out Harry's House of Fitness, and he was excited. He had had to leave numerous other gyms in the past year, and he hoped this one would actually work out.

Gordy was gorgeous. No two ways about it...but a couple or three ways went through people's minds when they saw him.

He was also very sweet. The sweetest man in the world, by some accounts. But he wasn't too bright. That was a muscle stereotype that unfortunately applied to Gordy.

Jerry and his crew noticed (once they were able to avert their eyes from the Herculean-sized Adonis) that everyone who could see Gordy in the gym was flustered, swooning. Most notably, the women who Jerry and his friends always strutted for were now totally oblivious to their presence and drawn to this new mountain of muscle. Jerry, of course, got very jealous.

Gordy went to the dumbbells, parting the foursome, nodding pleasantly at them. They forgot to nod back. There wasn't room for a nod with all that muscle in the area. Gordy did 50-pound dumbbell curls as a warm up. One of Jerry's friends gasped. As he did his set, Gordy's tight shorts constricted the two mounds of muscle ass so tight that it looked as if he were carrying two large melons in his shorts.

Jerry was getting more jealous. His own ass had always been the best in the gym. The girls had always told him so.

Filled with discontent, Jerry walked to the cables, intent on doing cable rope extensions until Gordy left the free weight area. He couldn't compete with that. Even the gay guys at the gym, whom Jerry never really associated with, would be drawn to Gordy. And while Jerry didn't want to have sex with another man, he wanted to keep their attention. But again, with an ass like that, how could he compete?

"Why am I thinking about his ass?" he chided himself as he leaned over to get the rope that was lying under a weighted barbell.

The rope, however, was caught. Jerry could not get it out from under the barbell without lifting the weights. But the weight added on was too much, even for him. He thought for a milli-second about asking Gordy, but would not be able to stand the mocking eyes of his friends. So, he decided instead to remove the collars, then whittle the weight down to a manageable size. He could then lift the barbell off the rope himself. Of course, it never occurred to Jerry to just do another exercise. He was stubborn and set and distracted.

Jerry twisted and pulled, but the collars would not give. He tried again, but they wouldn't so much as budge an inch. At this, he began to get angry at every person in the gym, even though none of them aside from Gordy could have possibly used the heavy problem-causing barbell.

"Can I help?"

Jerry looked up to see Gordy standing a few feet away, his face pleasant and grinning. Jerry's three friends watched, still awestruck from behind. One of them kept staring at Gordy's ass. Was he gay? Jerry had nothing against gay guys, but it would be weird for him if one of his friends, his workout buddies, was gay. They had all seen him naked, watched him pose naked.

"Why did we pose naked?" he asked himself.

"With the weights," Gordy reiterated. "Do you need any help?" His voice was nice and calm. Not the harsh, heavy affectation of most gym rats and bodybuilders.

Before Jerry could say no, Gordy cast his considerable shadow over where Jerry stood and bent over to take a look at the collars on the barbell. Making room for Gordy's mass, Jerry had been forced to position himself directly behind the new muscle god. When Gordy bent over to work on the collars, he incidentally pushed Jerry against the mirrored wall with his massive bum.

Jerry's friends' expressions changed to faces of shock and some excitement, but Jerry wasn't watching them. He was busy trying to quell the rising feeling of his own confusing excitement down below. The little green shorts holding the big, big melons began to flex and rub Jerry's crotch as Gordy twisted and turned the collar on the barbell. Gordy grunted in labor as he worked, and this only added to Jerry's horrific predicament. His dick became harder and harder as Gordy's ass massaged him.

Pressure, release, pressure, release. Grunt.

Every so often Gordy would shift in his stance, and this would enhance the unwanted pleasure Jerry was feeling. Gordy's ass began to rub Jerry faster and harder as the monster loosened the collars.

Pressure, release.

At last, Jerry couldn't control himself any longer. The huge mounds of greenclad ass were now the most beautiful things he had ever seen. He grabbed them, pushing into Gordy with force. But Gordy merely thought Jerry was trying to help. He encouraged him.

"You got it, buddy! That's it!"

Jerry came just as Gordy rose to an upright position.

"That should do it!" Gordy exclaimed.

Jerry gasped and moaned, barely able to stand against the wall. "Th-thanks."

"Not a problem," Gordy said, walking away.

Across the weight room Jerry saw his friends, seated now, knees close together, hands over their crotches. From the looks on their faces he knew he was safe.

They would never, ever talk about this. EVER.

Eric Arvin

Gordy Squats Down Low

MIKE was a man of layered secrets. His secrets had secrets. He was married to a lovely woman, but without her knowledge he was also sleeping with another man. And without that man's knowledge Mike was sleeping with even more men. He had seen an episode of Oprah about what he did. Oprah didn't understand. Men found him adorable. He reciprocated that. But he couldn't let the world know the truth. The world would topple like a top-heavy weight rack.

Mike sat on the bench, ready to get to work on some hardcore chest pumping. He loved chest day. His boyfriends loved his chest, though his wife, who now shot him an adoring glance from an elliptical, thought she was the only one to enjoy its wide expanse. His pectoral plains.

He had heard tales of a new gym member here at Harry's House of Fitness. A guy who had caused quite a stir. Apparently he had been so formidable that even the four horse's asses, who hollered and carried on in the free weight area, were hushed. They worked out at different times of the day now. Mike couldn't see how one man could silence those idiots...

But then, in walked Gordy in his tight green shorts.

Gordy was happy. It was leg day. Gordy loved leg day. He loved it because his legs always responded so well to the strenuous workouts he put them through. He didn't know why he grew muscle so easily, but he did. He always had. And that muscle had been his ticket to great friends and good times. His innocence was his only stumbling block.

Mike watched the behemoth approach, but looked away when Gordy smiled at him. Mike could feel his blood start to grow warm, to enliven certain desires. He thought of his wife so nearby, and laid down to do his first set of presses. The pressure in his pants was distracting, though, and he had a difficult time concentrating on anything. Still, he calmed himself. It was just a man, a big man, but a man just the same. Mike had been with dozens of hot men.

When Mike rose from his unsatisfactory first set, his dick immediately went hard. He was powerless to stop it. Gordy was directly in front of him at the squat rack, bending over, stretching. His ass full and round. Lyrics to hip hop songs filled Mike's head. Gordy's tiny shorts nearly disappeared into the crevasse between his firm cheeks. He stacked the bar with a hefty amount of weight and called it a warm up. As he did his squats perfectly, lateral, even, Mike nearly came in his shorts. The sight of those thighs, of that ass! He felt dizzy. He shook his head and would have gone elsewhere if it were not for the very noticeable extension jutting out in front of him like a sign leading the way.

"Can I get a spot here in a minute?" Gordy asked politely.

"Uh...um." What was he to do? He didn't want to be rude. If there was a chance he could possibly get this guy into bed he didn't want to spoil it by refusing to spot him.

Thankfully, his penis had subsided just a bit as Gordy piled more and more weight onto the bar. Mike simply looked elsewhere to distract himself from the green shorts. To his wife on the treadmill now.

Gordy let him know he was ready by a nod, then turned about and positioned himself under the bar. Mike quickly stood and walked to the squat rack, praying no one had noticed the growth in his workout shorts.

The bar bowed as Gordy lifted it. Mike thought it might break. There weren't enough weights in the gym for Hercules.

"I need you to stay real close," Gordy instructed.

Mike nervously, not without glee, leaned himself against Gordy. He felt his cock lying against Gordy's back, ready to explode. As Gordy made his first descent, Mike came upon a startling realization: his dick had fallen into the crevasse! There was no hope now. All hope to avoid humiliation was lost.

Gordy rose, tightly enfolding Mike's thickness in his ass. Down again, up again. Mike was getting woozy, feeling the heat from his body, enjoying the unexpected friction. With as much weight as was on the bar, Mike expected Gordy to stop at four sets – but he kept going. Breathing hard. Groaning.

The friction took hold of Mike. An environment of surrealness, pleasure, set in. He didn't care who was watching. Let them see the most intensely erotic moment he had ever experienced. He grabbed onto the undersides of Gordy's arms and pressed his dick willfully into the crevasse. There was no going back. He was cumming.

Glory! Glory! Glory!

Gordy replaced the bar on the rack. Mike stepped back so as not to trip the man, but that was about all he could do. He stumbled backward, taking a seat on one of the benches. That was the best sex he had ever had.

"Thanks," Gordy said. "But next time, don't help me as much in those last few. Felt like you were almost pushing me up."

He walked away, the crevasse of ecstasy waving goodbye.

Mike hadn't yet noticed that someone had been watching the whole thing. Someone who was none too pleased. A young man. The same young man Mike had been on the down low with.

"Mike!" the man yelled. "You asshole!"

Mike's wife, distracted from her workout by her husband's name, climbed off the exercise bike and came to him. "Mike. Who is this man? What did you do?" Then, "Why are your shorts wet in the front?"

Eric Arvin

Gordy Takes a Shower

Gordy loved showering after a hard workout. It was a well-earned reward. He loved his muscles, each one; lovingly massaging each like a precious, fleshy jewel. And his muscles loved him, tightening up as he ran his soapy hands over them; hugging to his frame all the tighter. His was a happy body. When he stepped from the shower, the beads of water refused to leave, hiding comfortably in the valleys and dimples of his sublimely sculpted physique. Gordy never rushed the shower experience. His body deserved the pleasure after what it did for him. His nipples were perky with contentment as he strode steaming and sans towel into the locker area from the shower, whistling off-tune and oblivious to the small group of men assembled there.

Gordy had been a member of Harry's House of Fitness for only a week, and already his reputation had reached the ear of every gym member there. They all wanted to see him with their own eyes. Gordy thought the locker room exceptionally crowded, but thought nothing strange about it. He smiled, his placid cock and large balls swaying as his thick thighs bounced them back and forth.

Thigh to thigh. Thigh to thigh.

The other guys in the locker room could not help but watch Gordy's overripe manhood with jealousy and (disturbingly to most of them because for the most part they considered themselves completely hetero) a kind of lust. None of them were willing to admit this fact to each other, though. They made excuses, for themselves and their friends.

"His chest, man. I want to see his chest. Maybe he can give me some pointers."

"His legs. Yeah, his legs. I've always had a problem building my legs."

"His ass – I mean, hamstrings!"

They all knew the truth, though. As much as they refused to see it head on, so to speak, they were all crushing a bit on Gordy.

The group of men pretended to be busy going through their workout bags, or fixing their iPods, or spending an exorbitant amount of time slipping on a sock or off a shoe. Pretense hung in the air like humidity after a shower.

Gordy turned to his locker, his amazing, globular, frustratingly het-confusing ass shining smooth and...

"Juicy," someone whispered. Everyone heard it, but no one snickered or looked to see who had said it. They were all thinking the same thing anyway.

They admired the muscles in Gordy's back as he continued to dry himself. They refused to look anywhere but at Gordy. They refused not because Gordy was so stunning (which he was), but because if they did look around they knew they would have probably seen their buddies' pricks going hard...just like their own. Things were disturbing enough without an orgy erupting.

They were men. Surely straight men could control their own urges. Surely.

But none had counted on what happened next.

Gordy hadn't put his gym bag in the top of the locker; he had laid it on the bottom. To the audience's horror – or exhilaration – he bent down to retrieve it. The fleshen boulders spread. Muscular gates. The eyes in the room widened in dread spiked with anticipation. Each wondered, would they have enjoyed it if they were the recipients of a one-man show?

Just rise! Just stand up straight! The thought seemed to spread through the air, though unspoken. *Stand up, and we'll be fine.*

But something was wrong. Gordy's gym bag was caught. It was too large for the locker. How he had gotten all that in there was anybody's guess. Much like Gordy fitting into his green shorts. He began tugging, pulling on the bag. His ass bumping up and down, muscles striating. Inviting.

"God, no!" someone whispered.

But the feel in the air now was Yes! Yes! Yes!

Gordy's ass bumped and jiggled and bounced teasingly. Eyes grew wide in fear, mouths wetted, gasps were heard aloud, and dicks shot up as if shot full of Viagra. It was an almost painful erection for each man there. Almost too much for their skin to hold.

Pounding on lockers could be heard as men fought their urges. Yet, they could not keep from staring at Gordy's unknowing booty bump.

Then, without so much as one man touching himself, they all began to cum. And not just streams, but eruptions. Violent and uncontrolled, reaching heights heretofore unknown in all of recorded cum-gushing history. Fountains and fountains from every last man. There arose from the group such a ruckus that Gordy at once stood and turned around.

The men before him sat or lay depleted on the floor and benches, balls drained dry. They were exhausted. Some hadn't even had a chance to work out yet. They were dripping their own cum and staring humiliated at Gordy.

Gordy's shoulders dropped in a kind of despair. "Darnit! Not again," he said. "I guess I have to find another gym, huh?"

As if answering a drill sergeant in short, stern unison, the men yelled pleadingly, "*No!*"

Eric Arvin

Other Titles by Eric Arvin

The Rest is Illusion by Eric Arvin
- ☐ **Paperback:** 196 pages
- ☐ **Publisher:** <u>Booklocker.com</u>, Inc. (September 29, 2006)
- ☐ **ISBN-13:** 978-1601450562

A coming of age story with a supernatural bent, *The Rest is Illusion* is set on the campus of Verona College, a small liberal arts school that overlooks an ancient river valley. The story centers on five students at critical points in their lives. Sarah, a young woman at odds with everything her parents stand for; Ash, a mysterious genius; Dashel, a young man with a mysterious illness; Tony, a closeted football star; and Wilder, a manipulative hopeful politician. Their individual stories run in and out of each other in the course of a week. Personal problems are further complicated by an unseen force that surrounds the college, living deep in the woods. As this entity begins to more fully touch the lives of the characters, things begin to unravel. For some this is a needed change, but for others this is a catalyst to a terrifying end.

SubSurdity: Vignettes from Jasper Lane by Eric Arvin
- ☐ **Paperback:** 158 pages
- ☐ **Publisher:** iUniverse, Inc. (June 21, 2007)
- ☐ **ISBN-13:** 978-0595454822

Jasper Lane is the perfect, sunny, American neighborhood, or so it would seem. Melinda Gold is a young mother whose desire for position in the neighborhood is at odds with her upbringing by her ultra conservative mother. The same mother who makes life hell for Melinda's son, Patrick; Cassie Bloom is the grand dame of Jasper Lane, living on a cul du sac and doing her best to annoy Melinda. But she has a secret of her own regarding her missing husband and son that only a few, including the transsexual Vera, know about; Rick has just moved into the neighborhood and has immediately fallen for the ex-Army man, James. Will he find the courage to go after what he wants? Terrence, Rick's good friend, has found out he has a son from a one-night stand years before where he dallied with heterosexuality; and the perfect couple Steve and Sandy have run into a rough patch which forces Steve to find employment in the porn industry.

All these stories interlock and play out in a brightly comic way with gay porn parties, sexually confused animals, and dead bodies all being thrown in the mix. It may not be perfect, but it sure is fun!

Other Novels from Dreamspinner Press

A Summer Place by Ariel Tachna   248 pages
Paperback $11.99   **eBook** $5.99
ISBN: 978-0-9795048-4-6   **ISBN**: 978-0-9795048-5-3

Overseer Nicolas Wells had been coming to Mount Desert Island for ten summers to help build cottages for the rich and powerful. Despite his secrets, he had grown comfortable in the peaceful little island town, getting to know its inhabitants and even to consider some of them friends. The eleventh year, however, he arrived to startling news: the island's peace had been shattered by a murder. At the request of the sheriff, Shawn Parnell, Nicolas agreed to hire Philip Hall, the local blacksmith and the probable next victim, in the hope that the secure construction site would be safer than his house in the village. He never expected the decision to lead to danger. Or to love.

Cursed by Rhianne Aile   232 pages
Paperback $11.99   **eBook** $5.99
ISBN: 978-0-9795048-2-2   **ISBN**: 978-0-9795048-3-9

Upon their grandmother's death, Tristan Northland and his twin, Will, come into possession of her Book of Shadows and the knowledge that their family is responsible for a centuries old curse. Determined to right the ancient wrong, Tristan sets off across the ocean to reverse the dark magic that affects the Sterling family to this day.

Benjamin Sterling might not be happy with his life, but it is predictable – at least until Tristan Northland shows up in his office, unannounced and with nowhere to stay. He has plenty of reason to distrust witches and Northlands, but instead of caution, he experiences two unexpected emotions: hope and love

To Love a Cowboy by Rhianne Aile   228 pages
Paperback $11.99   **eBook** $5.99
ISBN: 978-0-9795048-8-4   **ISBN**: 978-0-9795048-9-1

Seven years ago, Roan Bucklin left the family ranch for college, leaving foreman Patrick Lassiter with a mix of sweltering emotions: relief, regret, and nearly overwhelming desire. Afraid that Roan would regret giving himself to an older man, Patrick let him go without a word about his true feelings. But Roan took Patrick's heart with him.

Roan had harbored a crush on Patrick from the time he'd turned fourteen. He thought he'd gotten over it, grown up, moved on, but now he's back and home to stay. After one look, he knows he has something to prove to Patrick – that he wants to be claimed by the cowboy who has always possessed his heart.

www.dreamspinnerpress.com

Size Matters: Short Stories Long Enough to Satisfy
A Dreamspinner Anthology of Gay Erotic Novellas
Paperback $20.00   eBook $12.00
ISBN: 978-0-9795048-0-8   **ISBN**: 978-0-9795048-1-5

Snowfall In Seattle by **Lucia Logan**
Christopher Booth was just helping out a co-worker, never expecting it to catapult him into the spotlight. When he needs help himself in his new job as the host of a radio sex advice show, he shares some private secrets that lead his longtime friend, Neal Kenelly, to see him in a new light. However, Neal's past makes him leery of approaching the other man openly. Will a more subtle approach be enough to win him Chris's heart?

Healing In His Wings by **Ariel Tachna**
When the crew of the *Starfire* is struck by a mysterious plague, help comes from an unexpected source: the healers of a nearby planet. First Officer Ryan Nelson is sent to act as liaison officer between the Petari and the *Starfire* and finds unexpected healing in their tender care.

Ever Changing by **Shay Kincaid**
Born a Changeling, Chase Spencer had fooled his teachers, playmates, even his parents with his altered appearances, but as he reached adulthood, the games took on a whole new meaning. Each weekend it was a different 'persona' and a different partner, and that seemed to suit the young man just fine, until the night he set his sights on someone from his past. Will Chase emerge from his latest game unscathed, or will he be caught in a web of his own devising?

Dreamscape International by **Connie Bailey & Rhianne Aile**
Visiting dreams to grant paid-for wishes, Dreamwalker Lucien Clarke is the best at navigating the twists and turns of sleeping minds. While recovering from a job gone wrong, he discovers that fantasy's passion just can't match reality's love. Will unseen dangers ruin it all?

An Academic Dilemma by **Alix Bekins**
Rodrigo is an art history student who finds himself attracted to a new friend while also undeniably drawn to his professor. Exploring his feelings for them both leads him into a strange new world of trust, kink and surprising secrets.

www.dreamspinnerpress.com

Size Still Matters: Short Stories Still Long Enough to Satisfy
A Dreamspinner Anthology of Gay Erotic Novellas
Paperback $20.00   eBook $12.00
ISBN: 978-0-9801018-2-9   ISBN: 978-0-9801018-3-6

Sight Unseen by Shay Kincaid

Famous actor Jackson Prescott wonders if anyone will ever look past the glitz and glamour of his Hollywood persona and love the person behind the name. So after accidentally dialing a wrong number and feeling an instant attraction to Devon Forrester, the stranger on the other end of the line, he decides to test the waters ... using a different name. After getting to know Devon through their daily phone calls, Jackson starts to worry: Will the relationship they've built crumble when they meet face to face? Or will Devon be able to forgive Jackson's deceit?

Take My Picture by Giselle Ellis

Aaron has no idea what he's walking into when he shows up to pose for a famous photographer. Instead of being the focus of the camera, he ends up working as Jake's assistant. Five frustrating, thrilling and crazy years later, Jake discovers Aaron has become the focus of his life, a life that's threatened when Aaron finds someone else, and Jake has to set his beloved muse free.

Start From the Beginning by Chrissy Munder

A heart attack leaves Miles wrangling with a slow recovery and a quiet retreat ... just one cabin down from wounded warrior Drew. Although he's unhappy to have his solitude invaded, Drew finds himself fascinated with Miles, but he can't bring himself to push aside his skittish nerves. Both men fear rejection for different reasons, but what if they've instead found the acceptance they crave?

Evan's Heaven by Nicki Bennett

Actor MacAlester Kerr wanders into a whole new world of pampering and pleasure when his director sends him to *Evan's Heaven* for a pedicure. Right off, he meets *the* Evan and finds himself head over heels. Mac's on Cloud Nine when he finds out Evan feels the same.

www.dreamspinnerpress.com

Desire Beyond Death: Tales of Eternal Love
A Dreamspinner Anthology of Gay Erotic Novellas

Paperback $20.00   **eBook** $12.00
ISBN: 978-0-9801018-4-3   **ISBN**: 978-0-9801018-5-0

Ink: The Tale of a Vampire in Melbourne by **Isabella Rowan**
   After too long alone, Dominic enters a tattoo parlor, desperate to find a way to reconnect to life. He meets Michael, an artist who evokes feelings and needs Dominic knows are dangerous. But those emotions and the allure of the handsome human intoxicate Dominic as much as the blood that keeps him alive, and he finds that he – usually the hunter - just can't resist giving in to his prey.

After the Storm by **Chrissy Munder**
   Angry and frustrated with his chronic illness, Vincent Poulsen moves into an old lighthouse to live out the few days he has left. After a dangerous collapse, he meets the ghostly Captain Cason, who shares stories of his distant past. In the process, Vincent stumbles over the tragedy that binds the captain to the lighthouse and his haunted memories. Then fate offers them both a chance to change the future… for better or for worse.

Revenant by **Connie Bailey**
   When Bo Andressen and his salvage crew contract a job in a crumbling castle, they walk into a mystery of murder, intrigue, hidden treasure and greed that has its roots in the far past. Ghosts are only the first suspected danger – the crew, local constable Gavin Gilroy, castle owner Sir Rhys Turcotte and psychic Tristan Andrews have to find out who of a more earthly nature is involved, before more people fall victim to an ancient spectre who seeks to rejoin and conquer the mortal world.

Seeing is Believing by **Abigail Roux**
   Scott Cunningham has a ghost problem, a problem that requires a specialized touch. Enter Zacharias, Leo, and Andy – professionals, if you will – in solving said problems. But solutions don't always come easy, and if Zacharias and his crew can't get the job done, someone innocent might get hurt.

Bittersweet by **Madeleine Urban**
   His business failing and his marriage floundering, Harrison Holden is falling apart. To make things worse, he wakes one morning to see Piers Claybrook, a man he rescued after a car crash the night before, standing in front of him – the same Piers he'd seen dead in the hospital. Now a ghost, Piers believes he's with Harrison to make a difference in the other man's life, and it's up to the two of them to find the key to living – and dying – and how to walk the line in between without being separated by it.

www.dreamspinnerpress.com

www.ingramcontent.com/pod-product-compliance
Lightning Source LLC
Chambersburg PA
CBHW071333250626
47159CB00004B/1587